EMERGENCE

Published in 2023 by Hardie Grant Books, an imprint of Hardie Grant Publishing

Hardie Grant Books (Melbourne)
Wurundjeri Country
Building 1, 658 Church Street
Richmond, Victoria 3121

Hardie Grant Books (London)
5th & 6th Floors
52–54 Southwark Street
London SE1 1UN

hardiegrant.com/books

Hardie Grant acknowledges the Traditional Owners of the Country on which we work, the Wurundjeri People of the Kulin Nation and the Gadigal People of the Eora Nation, and recognises their continuing connection to the land, waters and culture. We pay our respects to their Elders past and present.

 A catalogue record for this book is available from the National Library of Australia

Emergence
ISBN 978 1 74379 996 3

10 9 8 7 6 5 4 3 2 1

Publisher: Pam Brewster
Managing Editor: Loran McDougall
Project Editor: Antonietta Melideo
Editor: Marg Bowman
Design Manager: Kristin Thomas
Cover and Text Designer: Celia Mance
Production Manager: Todd Rechner

Typeset in 12.5/18 pt Adobe Garamond Pro by Post Pre-Press Group
Printed in Australia by Griffin Press, an Accredited ISO AS/NZS 14001 Environmental Management System printer

EMERGENCE

The 30 best new voices with powerful must-read stories

Hardie Grant

BOOKS

Contents

Foreword

For the third year running, Australia has once again proven that it's home to some of the most talented and passionate voices writing has to offer. The SBS Emerging Writers' Competition received thousands of short stories speaking to this year's theme of 'Emergence', with each new memoir as diverse as they were affecting. From stories that begin across the globe detailing the realities of Assyrian migrants, to the pain and perseverance of First Nations Communities right here at home, this year's anthology reminds us that lives that exist on the margins are entire worlds in their own right.

The thirty shortlisted stories housed in these pages are a masterclass of not only skill and style, but of tenacity and raw integrity. Each world you will be taken to will hopefully remind you, as it did for us, that all literature is conversation, a dialogue between reality as it is and reality as it could be. You will find stories of incredible grief and fear, but also of hopefulness and levity. We hope their beauty stuns you as much as it stunned us.

There is no greater example of these wonderful contradictions than this year's winner, *The usual* by Tessa Piper. The familiar scene within a suburban family home on a spring day is distorted beyond recognition, and yet it feels anything but foreign. The implications of Piper's words echo eerily long after reading, and provide just one example of the astonishing talent that has been unearthed through the competition this year. And she's in good company – prize winners Monikka Eliah's work *Cabbage*, Gemma Tamock's *Call and response*, Alexander Burton's *The lanyard is my superpower* and Sidney Norris's *Cicada* are vignettes that could not be more distinct from one another, but all share a common humanity and willingness to give.

In a country as diverse as this one, we need writers like the thirty you're about to discover. We need their honesty and their determination. We need these stories.

—*Judges Alice Pung and Christos Tsiolkas*

The usual

Tessa Piper

In the crumbling red-brick, black-mould flats near the station, preparations are underway for another piss-up.

Mum and Dad are still sulking and snarling after last night's argument, but are showing small signs of resolve as the afternoon's promise of a drink and whatever else edges closer.

It's the first day of spring and warmer than it should be.

In years to come, hot spring days like this will hit me sharp in the face like a warning, but today I fall easily into Mum and Dad's slipstream and get to work packing my textas from the coffee table and pouring crisps into plastic bowls.

At some point in the afternoon, the adults pile into the lounge room, faces and fingertips hardened from too many late-night gigs in Sydney's pubs, bellies bloated from the grog catching up with them.

Guitars and longnecks in hand, they rough my hair, ask the same questions: 'How are you, love?' (Good)

'How's school?' (OK)

'Got yourself a boyfriend yet?' (Yuck, no)

Soon they're rolling joints and tuning guitars and pissing themselves laughing. It's always my favourite part. I sit on the worn carpet while they tell stories, shoving chips in my gob and watching Mum's face closely so I can laugh when she does, like we're in on the jokes together.

The adults start taking turns going in and out of Mum and Dad's bedroom and a billion tiny electrons charge the air in the flat.

Mum comes back from the bedroom, eyes wide and quick. She gets a can of Fanta from the fridge and hands it to me.

'Why don't you ride your bike and go and see if Whatshername down the road is home, love?' she yells over the music.

The party has barely started and I'm already a bloody hassle.

I get my bike from near the front door and choof off down the street. Me and the girl down the road sit cross legged out on the nature strip, slurping Fanta and pulling the bindi grass out in clumps. We thumb our way through old magazines until we start slapping mozzies and her mum calls her in for tea.

I ride the long way back and then up and down the street and past the flats a few times, pretending I don't live there and am just riding past. I do this sometimes: blink hard and try to see the flats like any passer-by would. Maybe their height makes them look grand. A red-brick castle of sorts. I decide the stained mattress out the front probably gives it away and plonk my bike down to the ground floor.

I hear and then smell that the party's ramped up. The reverberation from the guitar amp is making every poor bastard's windows rattle. The common area stinks like weed and reeking sour piss.

Someone will call the cops soon for sure.

I hold my breath as I wheel my bike into the flat and close the front door behind me. Entering the lounge room, the adults' faces freeze as plates and rolled-up notes are hurried behind backs too slowly.

I see Dad and one of the men at the table, faces colourless, heads nodding, ligaments slack. Their leaning bodies defy physics in slow motion.

The needle is cradled in Dad's hand. Mum bristles.

'I told you to go down the road!'

'They were having tea, Mum,' I say, scanning Dad for signs of life.

'Don't worry about him. You know what he's bloody like. It's your bedtime,' she says, and I scurry down the hallway to my room.

A little after midnight a knock at my bedroom window breaks me from an early dream. I turn my head sharply, but there's nothing there. I close my eyes, wide awake.

A second knock freezes me.

I hear laughter at the window and get out of bed tentatively. At the window I see the face of one of Dad's mates. He's ridden my bike around the back and is standing on the seat of the bike propped against the wall under the window.

He motions for me to slide the window open.

'Didn't scare you, did I?' He laughs, his breath stale with beer and smoke.

'Nah, course not!' I reply, my hands sweaty.

He puts his hands on the window ledge and jimmies himself up until he is high enough to swing one leg through the window, and then the other.

He's in my room.

He turns his back to me, looks out the bedroom windows to the backyard.

'You ever see people doing any funny shit?' he asks, motioning over at the windows of the flats facing ours.

'Nah, not really,' I say. 'Mostly old people in those flats.'

He turns back around to face me and steps closer.

'You know what?' he says, his eyes searching me. 'If you can see them, it means they can see you, too.'

I stare at the buttonhole of his shirt and trace the zigzag stitching with my eyes. I see the beat of his heart in the shirt's fibres.

He swallows.

'They don't know what they're missing, you know. Watching you from out there would be real special. I'd like that.'

Up the hall in the lounge room a glass smashes. Someone yells, 'Taxi!'

The adults shriek. Hilarious.

He grins.

'Better not forget your bike in the morning, kiddo,' he says. 'Wouldn't want it to get nicked.'

———

Mum and Dad still aren't up.

I'm lying on the floor in my room on the carpet, re-reading an old *Dolly* magazine for the umpteenth time.

The hot afternoon sun is streaming in. Last night's urine stain on my sheets is now bone dry.

Mum walks in. Retreats.

'Jesus, what died in here?'

'I wet the bed, Mum,' I say. 'Can you change the sheets?'

'For God's sake, Tess,' she says. 'Bit old for that now, aren't you?'

She walks over to the window and slides it over to let some air in. Sees my bike propped up against the bricks below.

'What the fuck is your bike doing down there?! Want it to get nicked, do you?'

I freeze, worried she can see me floating.

We're interrupted by a knock at the front door.

'COMING!' she yells, and we pad up the hallway.

It's one of the other men from last night. He goes to hand Mum something, but sees me behind her and keeps his fist tight. Mum's hand reaches to his. Their hands slide against each other, and Mum, receiving, closes her fist quickly, but I see it. The tiny plastic bag with the white stuff.

She nods at him.

He laughs. 'Told ya I'd pay ya back, sweetheart. Always keep me promises.' He heads off.

Mum hurries past me to the out-of-bounds bedroom Dad's still in.

I go back to my bedroom.

She's forgotten about the sheets.

I lay on the floor.

Eye off the windows.

––––

The usual:

Music loud. Walls yellow. Smoke thick.

The slamming of a neighbour's window.

The thwack of semi-flat bike tyres on concrete around the side.

Me: Alert. Standing by.

Dad: Colourless. Slack.

Mum: Shrieking. Busy.

The piercing squeak of bike brakes.

The pulsing, heady evening air.

The watching.

The urging.

The rest of them squawking at one of the comedians in the lounge room.

Hilarious.

Me: Dropping the towel, facing the window.

Him: Possessed and helpless. Raw and erect. Charged and arrested.

Unzipping, rubbing, frantic.

I have three secrets:

One: I can turn windows into mirrors. You can, too. First, stare through the window at his face. They like that. Now, very carefully, shift your gaze from him to the reflection of your small body in the glass. He'll disappear.

Two: I can make a monster. You can, too. You need to concentrate for this one. Stare at your face in the window's reflection and do not stop. Watch it start to shift and change. Watch the angles and shapes of your face blur and contort. Watch the monster come. He'll disappear.

Three: I can fly. You can, too. You don't have to try with this one. Feel your limbs buoyant with blood. Your cells, helium. Do what you will. There is no me. I disappear.

Release.

I slide the window and he jimmies in. Shallow, stinking, shaking breath.

Pupils dilated; our bodies forever captured by those windows.

His calloused fingers under my chin, gently lifting my shy gaze to meet his.

'Good girl,' he whispers.

'Good girl.'

'Good girl.'

He walks up the hall to the adults and I get into my bed and replay it over and over.

Him, learning my body. Me, learning it too.

———

Come sit with me here in the neon stars.

Can you see me down there in that room? The girl, preparing to dance.

See the windows, keeping only the elements out.

Sit with me here and press record. You and me: the silent observers, the future collaborators. When she's ready – a long time from now – we'll be here, pressing rewind and play for her a thousand times over.

See the others in the lounge room. Still chasing. Sad old bastards. Yellowed eyes and swollen guts.

Dad's not there. Hasn't been for a long time though.

See me look out those big windows and mark the steps of that old routine in my mind. How I learned over time to tilt and arch hips, how I learned to brush fingertips on nipples and stare into maddened eyes and how he'd put fingers in wet places to prove a point until I'd start to hover and then take flight.

See how it's muscle memory now.

Tonight though, there will be no dancing. They feel it too, the shift in the air.

See me step up onto the windowsill, the silhouette of my body stark and backlit.

See me slide the window open wide and move closer to the edge, curling my toes on the bricks and propping my hands to steady myself in the window frame as I dare to lean forward.

See me breathe in the still evening air surrounding those flats.

Watch long enough and they'll come, the monsters of the night. One by one, they'll find their way to that window, each man marking blazes as he comes, making the pathway up and through the window easier for the next.

They won't come tonight though.

See me dare to lift one hand off the frame, and lean further out of that window, the weight of my body entrusted in curled toes and gripped fingers.

Will I fall?

Yes. Over and over. My body and yours and hers and theirs and all of ours, never a match for the weight of the men and their secrets.

Watch as I teeter even closer to the edge, fingers starting to slip on the brick windowsill, my body dangling into the night.

Will I jump?

Yes. Over and over. Into wrong beds and mattresses propped up by milk crates, into dangerous infatuations stinking of shitty stale spirits, and into the arms of silver men gouging fingers in warm places.

I'll try, in those moments, head spinning, to take flight. Anything for one last chance to sit up here and play it over, searching for the moment where someone should have pressed pause.

Watch as I sit down on that window ledge, my bare legs and body emerging into the evening air. One foot and then the other reaching down to that old bike propped against the wall, the bricks scraping the skin on my back as I slide down and then propel myself with a jump to the concrete below.

See me swing one leg over the seat to sit on the bike.

See the secrets pour from our thighs.

See my bare feet on the pedals.

See me grip and push and glide.

See that empty room.

See me fly.

There's nothing here for the taking.

Cabbage

Monikka Eliah

Ato said the perfect cabbage would be bright green with crisp leaves tucked tightly in together, like it was keeping a secret. I found a bundled lime-coloured cabbage and held it up for her inspection. She shook her head – too small. She said she wanted a big one. A big one would have a mild flavour and be ideal for wrapping spiced rice and slivers of red meat. When I asked her how big, she pointed to her head. Ato had a big head. Her black hair bun was a golf ball in comparison. A big head meant a big face and Ato's face seemed to have more of everything: more cheeks, more chins, big eyes. She always wore a stark-pink blush and red lipstick, and right now under the fluorescent Franklins lights, Ato looked like the Disney drawings of Snow White.

I picked out a large cabbage and held it up towards her head for comparison. It was heavy and I had to use two hands. Ato clicked her tongue at me, grabbed the cabbage and used a square nail to point out fuzzy black spots across the base of it.

'La ah!' *No!* She insisted that if I didn't want them on my face, we wouldn't want them on the cabbage. I shivered at the image of black rot growing on my face. I hadn't seen this happen to any other seven year olds, but adults had all sorts of strange things growing out of their faces, so it seemed possible. Ato herself had three moles on her neck that looked large enough to start talking.

I watched her dig around in the crate and pull out three enormous cabbages. She squeezed them, checking their firmness. I copied her, giving the last one a knock like I had seen my mama do to watermelons.

'Chooga la bayet kha rakekha, balbich goo mardakhta,' she told me. *You never want one that's soft, it will turn to mush in the boiling.*

She picked up one of the three. Big, bright and firm. She held it with two hands at face height and had such a warm look in her eyes that, for a second, I thought Ato was going to French kiss the cabbage. Then she asked me if it looked like it had a good secret. I looked at how tightly the leaves were bundled and nodded.

'Perfect.' She rolled her 'r's when she said the word.

'Perfect,' I repeated. I said mine the Aussie way, where the 'r' sounded like an 'h'.

At the Franklins checkout, Ato held her cabbage instead of setting it down on the conveyor belt. She paid for it in stacks of ten cent coins and refused the plastic bag, insisting she could carry it under her arm. As we walked out of the store, past the clothing shop selling purple power suits and towards the front parking lot, Ato spotted her friend Linda. Linda was a face pincher and she liked to talk for a long time. She burned musky incense in her house and you could always smell it on her skin.

The scent made me dizzy as she reached out and squeezed my left cheek between her thumb and forefinger.

'Kma' shetrantah!' Linda squealed. *How pretty.* Ato nodded in agreement and patted me on the head. I pulled at the loose threads on the hem of my skirt while I waited for them to finish talking. Linda told Ato she was going to Franklins for groceries and then rolled her eyes into the back of her head. Linda hated Franklins and wished there was a Woolworths nearby. Ato laughed and agreed, Franklins was the worst. The shock of Ato saying this caused me to pull too swiftly on my skirt strings and I snapped them off.

I didn't understand why she was lying. Ato loved Franklins! Sometimes she came to Franklins just to walk through the aisles. This reminded me of my cousin hiding the 'No Frills' milk cartons in the laundry basket when her friends came over. I watched Linda nod along before she leaned in to whisper, 'Did you hear about Shmonee?'

I tried to contain my groan. This was definitely going to be a long chat. I looked around the shopping centre. The newsagency that sold 3D stickers was too far away to go on my own. Then I spotted a chef hat and moustache, Michel's Patisserie, just a metre away. Maybe I could look at their desserts while Ato spoke to Linda. I waited for a pause in the conversation to ask for permission, but there wasn't one.

Surely Ato would not mind. I'd be within eyesight. I walked over to Michel's. The buzzing of their refrigerated display case drowned out the other sounds of the shopping centre. There were three chocolate-covered cakes in the domed window. The first was covered in brown buttercream icing that separated where the caramel centre had started to drool out of the sponge. It had the words 'Happy Birthday' scrawled in cursive across the frothy top. The second had a white chocolate shell with a drizzle of dark on the top. The fat drops of ice magic around the base made it look like a melted candle. The third was the best: three tiers layered with cream, dusted with flakes of milk chocolate, topped with eight dollops of cream, each with a shiny red glacé cherry in the centre. I had never had a cherry but I had seen them in cartoons repeatedly plopped on the top of every sundae, cake, milkshake and cream pie.

I pressed my nose forward and held my hands against the glass. I wished I could smell the cakes. I wished I could sink my fingers into the soft sponge. I wished I could taste the grains of sugar and cocoa on my tongue. I turned around to ask Ato if we could buy one, but she was gone. I searched for her purple floral skirt and big head in the groups of women walking by, but I couldn't find them. My heart sank into my stomach. How could Ato leave me? What if we never found each other again? The strangers passing by started to look terrifying. Their voices too loud. Their heads too small. Their pimples, moles and skin tags coming towards me.

Where did Ato go? Did she leave the shopping centre? A woman with tan stockings, thin lips and dark-drawn eyebrows stopped and smiled at me. If Ato was Snow White, this woman was Queen Grimhilde. The woman was carrying heavy bags of groceries and one tore from the weight and spilled fruit at her feet. I didn't stop to check for a poisoned apple. I ran away from her and from Michel's, trying to think of where Ato had gone. Aside from the cabbage, I couldn't recall anything else she wanted to purchase today. Then I remembered what Linda had said about buying groceries. If I went to Franklins I would find Linda and she could help me find Ato. As I ran towards the big red 'F', I tried my best not to cry, but by the time I got to the entrance, the fear had swallowed me whole. I felt two fat tears roll down each cheek. Two tears gave way to four and the sniffling became useless against the snot running down my chin. I slipped through one of the checkout gates and saw a blond boy with a pink face sitting in his parents' trolley. He watched me crying and started to mimic me. He made his lips tremble and his eyes squint. He balled his hands into fists and twisted them in front of his face.

I felt the heat of embarrassment lick through my chest and turned to walk away from him.

I walked down each aisle carefully. Checking every adult's face for familiarity. Then I found her, Linda, with a half-full trolley, standing in the aisle that smelt like flowers. She was picking out a box of washing powder. I couldn't speak, I just stood in front of her trolley and cried. I was so relieved to see someone I knew. I didn't even mind when she pinched my cheeks and asked if I was okay. I shook my head. Then she asked if I was lost and I nodded. Linda told me she didn't have a mobile but she was sure if I stayed with her Ato would find us.

How? Bonnyrigg Plaza was huge. What if Ato didn't find me? What if I had to go and live with Linda? How would Mama and Baba feel? Could I live in an incense house and get my cheeks pinched every day? I saw a jar of chocolate spread in Linda's trolley. Maybe an incense house wouldn't be so bad. I looked over the rest of her trolley for more treats and saw the cabbage with the black spots under a dented Cornflakes box. Suddenly the thought of living with Linda became horrifying. The sadness that had been lulled by Linda started to bubble in my belly again. Then I heard someone screaming my name at the front of the store, and when

I turned to face their direction, I saw a glimpse of a golf ball bun. Was it her? As the groups of passers-by dwindled down to one or two, I saw Ato standing there waving the head of cabbage at me. I ran to her. Ducked under the metal gate that barred people from exiting and grabbed her around the legs, rubbing my tears and snot on her skirt. The bubbles of sadness popped and I felt soothed.

'Kamo shwiklakh gohtee?' *Why did you leave my side?* Ato asked, holding me by the shoulders and forcing me to face her.

I told her about the cakes in Michel's Patisserie and watched her nostrils flare. Then she started yelling at me. Yelling that I was terrible and naughty and careless. That she was so terrified she had lost me and so happy that she found me. Then she hugged me, pressing the cabbage between us.

On the drive home Ato insisted that I had given greys to her freshly dyed hair.

'Yimakh w' babakh tawiwah Ktililee!' *Your mother and father would have killed me!*

I sat with the cabbage in my lap. The edges of it, once crisp, were now wilted. The outside leaves had come undone. They hung free from the rest of the cabbage head. It had revealed its secret and I had missed it. When I asked my Ato what the secret was, she said, 'Kam amireh eka machkenakh.' *It told me where to find you.*

Call and response

Gemma Tamock

My mother often said, 'Never marry a man who can't dance.'

I feel that this advice would have been easier for me to take if I had not had the six-foot frame of a South Sea Islander. Latinos, and those drawn to salsa dancing in Australia, tend not to be anywhere near my height. I had previously spent many demoralising nights as a wallflower, and I didn't think I could ask a man to dance. Those were the patriarchal rules of the salsa dance floor.

If I did get a dance, I might come across some Aussie muppet who'd been to a couple of dance classes and who knew a sequence of moves, but couldn't lead. We would invariably come a cropper when he decided to put me into a double or triple spin with his 5 foot 9 body. The specific laws of physics around this – which I know without needing a degree – simply don't allow a man who is shorter than a woman to do that. I was often frustrated enough after one dance like this to call it an early night.

Then I danced with Joe.

Joe and I are quite a sight on the dance floor. Joe is no triple-turn fool. He is 5 foot 6 and knows how to dance with women taller than him, possibly because many women are. More importantly, he is a funster. There are no rules, only the joy of moving to great music.

'It flicks a switch on the inside.' It certainly does. Joe is lit when he dances.

We both gravitated towards Cuban salsa, which has fewer flashy spins than the salsa that developed in LA and New York. Cuban salsa is more fun, and many of the dance steps 'belong' to different Yoruba gods and goddesses – the African religion that the slaves took with them to the New World. We learned songs and dances that Cubans associated with Oshun and Yemaya – the goddesses of love and mothers respectively – and Changô, the god of thunder and drums.

So far, so culturally interesting. And then, a goddess appeared to me.

I was standing in the shower while a thunderstorm raged outside. It was late at night and I was alone in my Sydney flat. A voice spoke to me.

You are mine, the voice said.

'Oshun?'

I am yours.

At the time, I thought I had all the spirituality of a sock. But I knew a goddess when one was talking to me.

I am beauty. I am love. I am sex. I was not sure which of us was speaking in my head, but I think we were claiming each other. Was it really the Yoruba goddess of love talking to me?

I thought nothing of it. I had been drinking champagne, after all, which was Oshun's favourite beverage. But a few months later, Joe and I were travelling north from our Sydney flat to Byron Bay, stopping in at Dorrigo. We walked to the waterfall.

It's a huge tumble of water, and there's a large pool where people swim in its wake. It is magical, or, depending on your religious bent, spiritual. It evokes something deep in the memory, or in the subconscious. It is a need for prayer.

As I stood dwarfed by this huge waterfall, as inspiring as any cathedral, a sudden inspiration told me to stand apart from Joe and the others – visitors and locals – with my palms facing the wall of water.

I whispered a greeting because something in me knew she was there – Oshun.

You will have a child.

I leaped back as if I had been shot, and Joe came over to see if I was OK. I was too surprised to tell him about Oshun, and instead said something about the waterfall being too powerful, and that I shouldn't have opened myself up to it like that.

Why was she talking to me like this? Had I called to her by singing her songs and dancing her dances? I had never wanted children – I was the product of an unhappy childhood. I had already told Joe that I didn't want a family, even though I knew he did. What was going on?

I meditated on her words for years.

I'd had lots of practice at the arguments against having children: Who wants to be a brood mare? I used to think. Was it really what I thought of it, or was it a way of deflecting fear?

I certainly was afraid. Afraid of the discomfort of pregnancy, the danger of childbirth, the pain of breastfeeding. The fear of being abandoned and joining the single mother's brigade. I had no judgement on single mothers, but I didn't want to be forced to parent alone. And then there was the deep terror of having an impaired child who might struggle to survive, or even the catastrophe of one or both of us dying. There was, to my mind, a complete encyclopedia of things that could go wrong.

I found it hard to balance these very real fears with the joys of motherhood because I simply had no experience of them. I had no contact with babies or young children. I would occasionally play with other people's kids, but that doesn't prepare you for anything. I was good at it, and I loved talking to and working with children. I especially loved, as the truism went, giving them back at the end of the day.

I didn't talk about this with Joe. I stewed on it by myself, trying to decide if I could make myself want children. Was it OK to have a child for Joe because he wanted one? When I said that out loud, I knew it wasn't right, but it was kind of how I felt about it. Joe would be a great father, and I believed he'd never leave us. Perhaps that was enough.

And I had an absurd hope – that I could be a good mother. What I did know beyond a shadow of a doubt is that I wanted Joe to have a baby. I would have to trust in the universe, and I prayed to Oshun, that I could want a child, too.

I was still trying to decide whether I wanted children or not when Joe and I went to Cuba with a group of salsa dance enthusiasts. There were fourteen of us on a dance tour, and we spent the first week in Havana, sweating in a magnificent, crumbling colonial building that seemed to be otherwise unused.

Our first morning in magical Cuba, we danced everywhere – on the street corner at breakfast, outside the famous little bar La Bodeguita del Medio, in the foyer of a restaurant, in Parque Central. We danced so much I was chafing and couldn't do another turn. We found ourselves in Hemingway's favourite bar, El Floridita, drinking G&Ts as big as our heads, smoking a cigarillo we had scored off an American tourist and dancing to the all-girl band. I looked at the clock. It was 11 am. What a country!

At the end of the week, we learned that one of the local dancers we had met was a priest from the Santería religion of Cuba's slave descendants. The followers of Oshun and the other gods and goddesses.

Joe turned to me with a grin and said, 'Ask him if he can marry us.'

The priest said in Spanish, 'Come back tomorrow: wear white.'

The next morning, the priest picked us up in a bicycle-taxi and we were met by six women at a house in an inner suburb of Havana. There were flowers, perfume and rings – a lush offering in a spartan little apartment. We sat on two high stools in the room that doubled as a kitchen and living area, facing two of the women. One had the Bible and the other wielded candles, perfume and the floral garland. The ceremony was in Spanish, which I rendered into English as best I could, with the translation aids of rum and cigarettes. By the end, we were tied by a garland, and surrounded by all six women and a halo of perfume.

'You will have a child,' one of them said. I was very quiet. Another prophecy? 'You must throw the garland into the ocean. A gift to Yemaya. She is the goddess of seas and oceans, and she is the mother of mothers. Women who want a child ask for her blessing.'

Where were we going to be able to throw flowers into the

waves? Maybe we could organise a trip to the beach before we left Havana in two days' time?

At a ruined fort in Santiago de Cuba, we snuck off from the group we were travelling with and walked down many flights of steps until we reached the sea. We asked the goddess for her blessing, and together we threw the garland of white flowers into her churning waves.

Five years after Oshun's prophecy, I was eight months pregnant. I was steeling myself for the final month, when the thing I was most afraid of came into view – the birth itself. But I had less time than I anticipated to prepare, because our son wasn't growing well.

A scan showed that he was in the 4th percentile of growth. The obstetrician told us that my placenta was no longer giving enough nutrition and that he wanted to induce the baby three weeks before the due date. I freaked out.

I got in the car by myself and drove, needing to think. Barefoot on Maroubra Beach, I stared at the waves in the growing dusk and asked for guidance. I mouthed the words of a prayer. 'Help me, Yemaya.' I heard nothing and feared I was just a woman standing at the ocean's edge, alone.

Then I looked up, and I saw the vastness of the entire ocean, rather than just the waves directly in front of me. I marvelled at this wide ocean before me.

'Your power is just awesome,' I said to the goddess of the seas.

In my head, a voice replied, Surrender is your strength.

So I surrendered, and late on the morning of the induction, the doctors began a sterile, medicalised process that took away any control that I might have had over the birth. Nothing had happened by the early evening. They broke my waters and after twelve more fruitless hours, the doctors told me that if I didn't go into labour in another four, I'd need a caesarean.

I flew off the handle, and when I calmed down, I apologised to Joe. Perhaps my fear had chased the contractions away.

'The baby is coming one way or another, Gem,' he said. 'Do what you need to do.'

I stood in the middle of a white-painted room, surrounded by machines, fluorescent lights and procedure-driven nurses. A surgical birth I didn't want was imminent. If my power was awesome, as Yemaya had said, what could I do to wrest some agency back?

I started to sing. I remembered the words of the goddesses' songs and then the steps of their dances. Joe and I danced together for most of the next four hours. Oshun and Yemaya lent us their strength.

Finally, before the surgical team arrived, our son was born singing. Perhaps it was one of the songs that he heard me singing to the goddesses that helped me become his mother.

Did I call to them, first in longing and then in fear? Or was the voice in my head my intuition or subconscious all along? Either way, I'm grateful for the little chats.

And Joe and I will teach our boy to dance, in the hope it will bring him the same amount of joy that he has brought us.

The lanyard is my superpower

Alexander Luke Burton

A lanyard is a long cord worn around the neck. They sway with whistles, keys and ID cards. A man in a lanyard has a job. And that job usually won't include working with his hands. It means he isn't lazy, desperate or a bogan. Growing up, I don't think any of the men in my family wore a lanyard. And sometimes it was hard to find work. Yet it was thick, calloused hands that hugged me, lifted me, and dropped rissoles and steamed veggies on my plate. My dad's hands had thin black cracks running through them. They looked and felt like marble. I loved those hands. But if he'd been a stranger, I think those strong hands would've scared me.

Southern Tassie takes all sorts. My home town was half hippy, full of short-lived cafes and greenie dreams, and half old-world families, chock-full of old churches, old farms and old ideals. My parents sat somewhere in between. They were tree changers – mainlanders looking for a life with meaning. The safety of a suburban box plot and a steady income was done away with for somewhere fresh. Not so much for their sake, but for their five children. My older siblings and I got to grow up with paddocks, with grass stains and smiles, and duck poo between our toes. We got to learn how to wander and how to think in peace. We were grotty and our clothes had holes. But who would care? Our neighbours were pademelons, cows and apple trees.

Caring for the land was harder than my parents thought, of course. Good-paying jobs were hard to come by. Extracurriculars were too far away. My parents changed their standards instead of their plans. My dad's hands grew more cracks. I guess appreciating life was the point of my parents' country experiment. I got to appreciate the mice skittering around the fireplace, keeping themselves warm in the winter. Me and the mice had a lot in common, actually. Small, resourceful, at home in the grass, and quietly hoping to change the boundaries and find the warmth of society. Of course I loved my home, but I didn't choose it.

My dad did all kinds of jobs. For a while he was a grounds-keeper at a private school. It wasn't my school, but I knew the place well. I went with him in the mornings to help with the bins, opening the shutters of the cafeteria, and washing out the toilets. Then I'd go to my school for classes. There's more high-visibility workwear than lanyards in my family. I've walked with my brother in his high-vis hoodie, covered in his metal shavings and concrete stains. I've seen women cross the street to avoid us. When you look rough, you're the last person people sit next to on a crowded bus. The free space is nice, but you feel a little tainted. Maybe those high-vis colours look like a venomous snake or a poisonous plant.

A lanyard is a symbol. It's not exactly prestige, and if it's a symbol of power, it's only the power of the go-betweener. It sort of makes you white collar, bureaucratic or an entry-level system minion. It's about filling a role. But the conductor blows their whistle, the guard unlocks with their keys, the service person logs in with their ID. A lanyard's not a symbol like a crown, saying 'I'm the most important.' It says, 'I do something. I have a reason to be here.' That can be a lovely feeling.

I've always felt good reading symbols. It's the confidence you get when most of your family is dyslexic, and your mum needed a second pair of eyes for the CVs. She's proud all her kids look for different things, even if it means some parts of our lives get lost in translation. Her youngest put those symbols to work studying geography at university and, after a rough start, managed to stay there. Now I've been studying for so long I get to help with the teaching, too. They even gave me a lanyard.

You don't really know what you've missed until you find it. There's hidden power in a lanyard. I heard that someone with a ladder can walk into any building. It never felt true until I had an ID card around my neck, regardless of where the card is for. In the eyes of those around me, I've gone from a high school teenager to a model citizen. I was already the colour they liked, and now I look older and employed. On two occasions I forgot to top up my bus card. The first time, I didn't have my lanyard. The driver watched me carefully. He didn't say much and let me onboard like he was sidestepping an argument. On the other, he said, 'It's okay! You have someplace you need to be.' The lanyard is a superpower. Wear it, and it means someone wants you.

I share smiles and waves with other staff and lanyardeers from around the uni cafe. I don't even know who they are. Once security guards would eye my face, after hours, like a warning that if I did anything, they'd know it was me. Now they see the red cord and nod, imagining I'm on some important research project late in the evening, burning the midnight oil. The name of the university is printed on the lanyard, but regardless of where I am, on campus or on the street, people ask me for directions. I'm safe. I must be good at something. The lanyard is privilege manifested as a uniform.

It makes me fly, too. The lanyard flew me from southern Tasmania all the way to northern Europe. The altitude and oddity make me dizzy. The quiet, grass-stained Tassie boy got a golden ticket on a string and carried it from Berlin to London. It carried me all the way to a lecturer on the historic grounds of Cambridge University, where the sandstone towers look like ivory. I told him about my studies, and about my island, too. I told him that there are no passenger trains and not much more than half a million people, that we sometimes nod at passers-by even if they're strangers, and we all know someone who knows someone who knows anyone else on the island. I spoke with a warm heart, but he mistook me and excitedly jumped into the heated, beating pistons of examination. They were quaint subjects and convicts, and we were researchers.

At my brother's work, people pay out of pocket for bad knees and chipped teeth. It's all from crouching on the ground and grinders kicking back against their faces while they work. At my office, people pay out of pocket for bad backs and therapy, from sitting all day and reading nothing but bad news. You think I'm joking, but I'm not. Everyone's got recommendations for good therapists. It's not about which job is better or worse. But there's nothing glamorous when it comes to teaching about climate change. Behind the office door, the lanyard is slow doom. It's not chipped teeth, but I've seen a lot of people in lanyards cry. I know I've done it.

I study people trying to escape from climate change. Someday I'll have to tell them that they can't. Not even the tree changers, and not even in Tasmania. In the breaks in the day, I stand around the tearoom and chat about the new decorations, the latest stage production, and all the pretty monuments we've each seen on our travels. It's the bourgie stuff I've never cared about. But the lanyardeers cling to it like a lowest-common-denominator distraction. It's their escape from the high-stress monotonies of a cramped office, cramped time life.

This is the anxiocene. The age of anxiety. The lanyardeers are good people, and they've told me their strategies to get through the week. Yoga, running, going to the gym, close friends and family, drinking, medication, other drugs. Maybe it's because I'm the youngest person there, but I remember when it wasn't like this. The homely raggedness, the wide-open spaces, the paddocks, the mice warming themselves beside the fireplace. Wearing the lanyard is one half of the superpower. But the other half is taking it off. The boy with the duck poo between his toes re-emerges. Taking off the lanyard is my superpower.

I'm not jealous of the lanyardeers anymore. It would be a bit difficult, since I am one. I'm not the only one who can take the thing off, either. I love my lanyard because I love what I do. A colonial mouse flew to the old kingdom on the magic of a red strip of cloth. But it didn't stay there. I grew up on country. Country a lot older than the kingdom. I grew up being taught you could trust a stranger in a lanyard. But there's plenty of space for wilderness left underneath that cord. That's the double edge of a uniform. It's worn to conform. It hides what's underneath, but not just from the customers, passengers, civilians. It's a canopy below that ivory tower. Who knows what's mustering underneath. I think there are a lot more marsupial mice than we're supposed to realise. And we're readying ourselves. We've got apple crumble, blackberry jam, and dirty feet. Above us are the Southern Lights from our clear night skies. What do you say, are you a bush mouse too?

We're all just one warm fire away. We'll emerge from our burrows. You and me, we'll be there.

Cicada

Sidney Norris

There was a period of time when my mother lived at this caravan park with Teddy – the Jack Russell terrier I grew up with. You drove in straight off some two-lane country road to a herd of discoloured trailers and demountables on the bank of a floodable river. The small billboard welcoming you into the park promised 'affordable cabins' and a 'waterfront location', which is about as comprehensive a statement as saying that wolves have soft fur and social skills.

Beyond the billboard was a canopy of ghoulish trees straight out of a season of *True Detective*, and the accommodation options beneath them felt so eerily devoid of life that only the mud-splattered cars parked beside them said otherwise. There weren't any personal effects outside or aesthetic alterations, just the occasional ashtray or stolen milk crate. For an extra $40 a week, you could get a cabin with its own toilet and shower, saving you a walk across the park to the demountable that housed the reception desk. It was easy to tell which cabins had bathrooms by the wheels and steel frames that elevated them off the tall grass, rather than the hurried stacks of misshapen bricks provided to the even less financially fortunate. I only visited Teddy and my mother there once when I was twelve or thirteen. It could've just been an overnight stay or a whole weekend visit, but I only (barely) remember a single night.

Emergence

I was laying on the floor of the 'bedroom', gripping my
Walkman with both hands and desperately pretending to be
asleep. Or if I was lucky, actually fall asleep, do away with the
night and be saved by the advent of tomorrow. My mother was
looking for something. Calmly at first, but every repeated search
of the same handbag or kitchen cupboard was like another rock
thrown at a hornet's nest. The buzzing in her head perverted her
concern, twisting it into urgency, and then that urgency to mania.
I turned my Walkman up as loud as I could handle it, but I could
still hear her obsessive mutterings moving through the space.
I didn't have Pearl Jam to protect me, or Funkadelic, or System
of a Down. For some reason, I was listening to a Ben Lee album,
of all things. I didn't even like his music that much but it was the
only line of defence I had against being present in that caravan.
Teddy was always such a pillar of comfort in moments like that,
but he was outside, sleeping in my mother's car. She told me he
liked it there.

Eventually, she pulled me up off the ground and told me we
needed to go to the police to report that someone had stolen
her medication. We couldn't drive there though because her car
hadn't been registered for who knows how long, so we walked.
I remember walking for a long time. Longer than what would be
considered reasonable in the dead of night at the behest of my
mother's paranoia. Looking it up now, Google Maps is telling me
that the nearest police station was an hour and sixteen minutes
away by foot. I don't remember if we got there. I don't even know
if we were ever heading there to begin with. The last thing I recall
is my mother's moonlit silhouette walking down the middle of the

highway, arms twisting into purposeful shapes above her head as if she was marshalling an aircraft that only she could see.

There's a certain amount of context needed whenever I go to talk about my childhood. It's annoying more than upsetting at this point. I feel like I need to carry around a book of footnotes and end every anecdote with a verbal asterisk. A few years prior to that night, my mother had descended into some sort of semi-functional psychosis. I've never been privy to the exact reason why, whether it be the drugs or the divorce or some insurmountable collection of stressors, but it left her unpredictable and often completely at odds with my reality. She would talk without pause in the absence of an audience. She would dance without music. She would have me help her self-harm in order to fulfil some invented need. She would write letters to museums in Egypt with the hope of obtaining a sample of Nefertiti's blood to appease the alien siblings she was set to marry. I know how that sounds and I don't mean to be flippant about it – these are just the kind of footnotes that help me translate my formative years.

That night was an example of how she would often take me places against my will. National parks, cemeteries, prisons. Anywhere that she thought we needed to be, according to whoever was speaking to her that day. Sometimes she wouldn't need to force me at all. I was such a fearful kid that as soon as I heard the particular tone and aural texture of her keys jingling, it triggered some kind of Pavlovian response that compelled me to join her, especially if I knew she was taking Teddy with her.

I definitely didn't want to go with her that night. I wish I could remember how it ended. I wish I could remember how a lot of those nights ended. My memory's kind of like the Notes app on a film student's iPhone – just an ever-scrolling list of engaging premises with no resolutions. It can be a comforting notion if I choose to look at it that way. My brain was looking out for me when no one else was, but it couldn't protect me from everything.

I remember exactly where I was when my mother called me and told me that Teddy had been killed. I had just spent the afternoon watching a high school girlfriend's netball game. I left alone and as I was walking between the petrol pumps of a nearby service station, my phone rang. My mother was in tears, saying that someone had firebombed her car overnight.

It wasn't clear if the arsonist knew that Teddy was sleeping inside at the time or if they were just looking to cause some property damage. Was it random? Was it personal? Had my mother's medication actually been stolen the night I was with her at the caravan park and she inadvertently kick-started a crescendo of retaliations with our late-night trip to the police station? She didn't elaborate much on the reason for Teddy's death, whether known or hypothesised, rather choosing to explain that it was the smoke that killed him, not the fire. I felt strangely reassured by that.

Though I'm sceptical of the details, I've never blamed my mother for Teddy's death. There have been too many other thoughts and feelings regarding her illness to contend with over the years. Occasionally an objective truth gets stuck in my teeth and I try to feel some level of sympathy for her. I'm her only child, after all, and I can clearly see now the consequences she's paid for her madness. The guilt that destroys her and the desperation she has to be a mother. My mother. I can see all of it and yet I will never be her saviour.

You tend to hope that these kinds of stories end with some form of forgiveness or reconciliation, but my path of healing has led me to a place of comfort through distance. I feel her effects on me every day as it is. Whenever my partner's voice raises to a certain volume in public, one that is completely normal and reasonable, I shut down. Instantly, I'm teleported to some highway McDonald's where I'm hurriedly trying to place an order as my mother's irritated mumbling slowly turns into aimless screaming. Whenever I misplace something or forget what I was doing, I spiral into an urgent reassurance of my own sanity. I can't explain how supremely unideal that is when you have a memory as tattered as mine. Even when it comes to something like spirituality, I envy those who are able to embrace it, because as hard as I try, anything that isn't observable is just another product of my mother.

And now my partner is talking about us getting a dog. What if he runs away? What if he gets hurt? What if he suffocates in the boot of some derelict SUV?

Every day is another cross-examination of the reality I grew up in and the reality that is. I don't say that to be dismissive of my experiences – they are as real to me as the laptop I'm writing this on – but rather to highlight the dangers of complacency should I forget which reality is which. Self-loathing, depression, feelings of worthlessness and suicidal ideation – they are a reality born from my experiences, akin to a cocoon that has no intention of letting me out. And I spent a long time waiting for my metamorphosis in that cocoon. Some kind of transformation that would relieve me of my ugliness. After a while, those thoughts that I was enclosed within convinced me that my metamorphosis was in death. That's where I'd escape all the rotting silk and find whatever wings I could. But that didn't go to plan, obviously.

There were some people in my life at the time who cracked open that cocoon for me – pulled me out of my reality and into theirs. I thought that in order for me to feel better, I needed so many things to change. Different parents, a different past. I needed to feel as though everybody on Earth loved me. I needed to transform from a caterpillar into a butterfly. But when I went through my rehabilitation, I found out that there were other realities I could live in. Ones that didn't demand so much change. Ones that freed me from blame. Ones where I was allowed to love and be loved in return, but not by the world, just by one person who felt like the world. Of course, my cocoon keeps trying to re-spin itself around me. I assume it always will. Though, I see myself now as less like a butterfly emerging from a chrysalis and more like a cicada that has to break out of the same hardening shell every summer.

My mother and I didn't talk about Teddy again until recently. I realised that I had never asked her what had happened to his body after the incident. Did she take him to a vet? Did she bury him somewhere? Again, a strange reassurance washed over me when she told me that she put him in a small suitcase and floated him down the Hawkesbury. I don't think I'll ever know for sure if that's the entire truth of Teddy's final days, but, if it is, I hope he floated somewhere nice. Maybe some affluent family found him washed up near Barrenjoey Lighthouse and they buried him in a plot of luxurious Northern Beaches soil. That kind of reality works for me.

Tender rising

Taymin-lee Pagett

I know a lot of shame. The shame which comes with womanhood. The shame that comes with failing. The shame of all the places from where I've come. My first taste of being but a baby in my home, then again in childhood, and again in my adolescence. It lingers, the shame.

My home, growing up, was ever changing. Moving away from friends countless times was something like second nature to me. I know nothing of stability. The only constant I've ever known was my love for my family, and my love for writing.

Living in a predominantly female household is desirable; even now in my twenties, I feel more comfortable living with women. My stepfather, growing up, made me put up walls, handed me this fear of men and showed me why, and showed me how. How to hate a woman, and how to hate myself.

First it was Mum who copped it. He didn't know that my sisters and I were Indigenous.

My first taste of the shame that came with 'I didn't know they were coons!' It seems most of the houses I've lived in had thin walls, or not thin enough. It wasn't long before we experienced the rage. He broke my CDs, he gutted my favourite teddy and tied it to the ceiling of our garage. The garage where he'd showed me Metallica, the garage where he would smoke weed, and drink on his own.

This was the birthplace of my hatred. The seed he had planted grew so large it cast a shadow. I had spent so much time hiding in its tangled limbs and eating its fruits. I indulged in this anger, I listened to angry music, I placed angry marks on my body, and I indulged the angry man who created this space.

We lived in Far North Queensland for a couple of years, I was around fourteen to fifteen years old. Not only was I impressionable, I was carving the details of the woman I thought I wanted to be. It was a strange time. I was so very sad and living on the 'wild side'. I was always full, licking my fingers at the taste of recklessness. Sneaking out, doing drugs and meeting with boys. Everything was so exciting and lonely simultaneously.

My stepdad would work out on the fishing boats, and those months when he was working far away were when we all felt the closest. My sisters and I weren't fighting, my mum would laugh with us and be herself. It was sweet and it was these long months that shed light onto what had been happening in our home for a decade. A moment of clarity, with no external influence whispering in our ears and turning us on one another. His final return left only my broken iPod, raw skin, and four angry women.

We moved home to the Illawarra, where we struggled for housing for a little while. On couches, blow-up mattresses and cockroach-ridden bunk beds of emergency housing. We grew fond of our freedom. The freedom of speech and the freedom to have fun.

When I was sixteen years old, I attended a spiritual workshop with my friend and her dad. I had always been spiritual, having been exposed to tarot and astrology from a very young age, enchanted by the kind of guidance I would receive externally. We were asked to review our relationships: with the earth, with our parents, with ourselves.

I knew my place on this earth, this land I stand upon belongs to me and my ancestors. I knew my relationship with father figures was strained and toxic. I knew my relationship with my mother and siblings was a result of the abuse we endured together.

But come time to read into my relationship with myself, it felt rigid and blunt. It was unexpected, a teen who was so sure of herself, a girl with so much experience, in a place like this. Where hearts are open, and honesty is necessary. My notes reflected the masculine form which lived inside my bones since I was a child.

The only way I had ever confronted my trauma was through writing.

I started writing poetry the night I first saw a shooting star. On the driveway in the humid Cairns air. The skies amass in history, and what is to be foretold.

That night I basked in the divine. The knowing part of myself which longed for vulnerability.

I have denied myself liberation, through suppression.

The illusionary heart on the sleeve, to my friends, and my family. After all that I had borne in life, I thought I had come through unscathed.

My sisters would argue otherwise. There are many scars left, between three of us. Our beauty is unmatched, in emotional intelligence, humour, caring nature, and each of our faces. We are but a result of history and a reckoning of the future. Being raised as we were, both delicate and strong, it was a matter of pride. To never admit we were small in the hands of our abuser.

A new season had dawned. Crisp and brown fall the leaves of rage. Seems fitting: that it takes time to untangle my sister, who's seen too much. Seems fitting: that it takes time for my mother to reveal herself. Seems fitting: that I slowly reclaim the childhood that was stolen.

The anger had always been so close to spilling. Too much for one girl and too much for one family.

The shame still lingers, I don't want to admit I am weak. But my mother was as helpless as me. In that small blue house, in a small blue town, we held each other. We were never big on words. Always talking but never anything of importance. I can hear the shame that teeters on her trembling lips when she can't take it anymore. I can see it when my baby sister admits defeat. Defeat that she is not tough and unbreakable. The difference being she can admit it now. There is no silent war on our emotions anymore.

For us as women who have handled it all before, it doesn't have to be too much for one family. It has taken and will take some time for us to surrender to the 'helplessness' of human emotion. I want to be liberated of the guilt that comes with my justifiable sadness.

I've started to accept that I need them, and they need me just as much. I hope, one day, my mother can sob in my arms. I hope she can tell me everything and talk my ear off. As a woman, I hope I can bask in this tenderness, for the feminine will be starved no more.

Polyester

Betty Petrov

'Blue boy, bluey, smurf, where ya hiding?' the gang of scruffy Grade 4 boys would yell as they searched every corner of the school, like hungry wild dingoes sniffing out their prey. Duy would find a new hiding spot every lunch break in the hope he could eat his lunch in peace. He sat crouched in silence, too afraid to let a crumb drop, trapped in a bunker, just like his Vietnamese ancestors, waiting for the enemy.

Fifteen years later, Duy, who had anglicised his name to David, stood outside with me, hiding in the damp rear alley behind our Melbourne city office. I was trying to wolf down one more cigarette as we avoided the rain, and hypothermia.

'That shit's gonna kill you,' he yelled over the rain that pelted down on the tin roof above.

'It ain't gonna kill me, mate, my lungs have been wolfing in polyester fluffs since I was three months old, I've got special filters on these lungs.'

David, confused, asked, 'Why the heck were you eating polyester at three months old?'

'Tomorrow ... let's go back in before the boss tracks us down – I can't be fucked listening to his shit,' I whispered as we snuck back in through the rear door.

The next day, committed to our ritual, David and I stood in the alleyway, once again in the rain, and I told him the story of my fluffy lungs.

I was born in 1975, to eastern European immigrants. They came to Australia lured by stories of a better life: words written in letters by newly arrived, semi-literate immigrants and read to children in a faraway village as they sat by candlelight in the evening, excited by the crisp white envelope and Australian postage stamp that had travelled by ship across the world. Filled with stories of opportunities and wealth, these letters were the window to the world, to which no storybook could compare.

With an empty suitcase and a single 20 cent coin that had arrived in one of those white envelopes, my parents arrived in Australia in 1969. Cheap land and dodgy eastern European builders ensured them a brown brick-veneer house of their own in Melbourne's outer west. St Albans was so outer, the place still had septic tanks, stinking like ripe manure, cows roamed in the distant fields, clay earth would not yield vegetables as it had back in the old country and there was no job, hospital, shop or bus stop for kilometres. This was real life, little house on the prairie.

Unable to afford day care, and not trusting she could hand me over to anyone, my mother started to work as a seamstress from the garage. Sleepwear became her speciality, her bread and butter. So, at three months old, tucked away in a wicker bassinet perched beside her on a mountain of polyester cotton pyjamas, my introduction to the garage sweatshop had begun.

Polyester cotton fibres were thick in the air, covering everything in a layer of white down, like a light coating of morning snow.

My mother stitched in garment warning labels about choking hazards and fire danger, ensuring other people's children were safe – oblivious to the fact that her lungs and mine were being filled daily.

My parents came from places where, as children, they worked in the fields, picking tobacco at 4 am alongside their parents and other villagers to escape the gruelling summer heat. Babies slept on makeshift grass beds on cracked dry earth, while children as young as five were expected to work from dawn in the fields. Putting children to work was the norm.

My first official job was as a flipper of pyjama cuffs: the stretchy cuffs that go around your wrists and ankles to stop the pyjamas from riding up at night. Hundreds would pass through our hands weekly. They looked like a string of sausages sewn together, one after the other, with a few centimetres of thread joining them. My younger brother's job was to cut the thread and hand them over to me, for folding and flipping. Fortunately we could do this job after school while sitting in front of the TV watching cartoons, which made it somewhat bearable. The cuffs were organised on large trays and delivered back to my mother in the garage, where another 10 metres of cuffs would be picked up. A never-ending stream of sausage cuffs.

I learned to sew at age eight. At first, all the threads were removed and I would go at full speed, with the industrial overlocker banging away. I learned to go straight and fast, and not to cut off too much fabric, or my fingers. By age twelve I could assemble, undertake quality control, hang, label and tag, organise according to the job sheet and have hundreds of pyjamas ready for the delivery truck.

School holidays were the worst. We were trapped; layers of fibre would stick to our sweaty skin, to be scraped off like a snake shedding skin, before going to sleep. As we worked, we would hear the neighbourhood children laughing and playing in the streets on their bikes, drinking hot water from garden hoses, cooling off under sprinklers and slurping on icy poles from the local milk bar.

We were stuck in a sweltering garage, with only a corrugated tin roof protecting us from the unforgiving sun. In the summer of '87, the heat became unbearable, so a rickety, second-hand brown Fujitsu air conditioner was installed. It hung on for dear life, wedged in a partially opened aluminium window, surrounded by cardboard patched together with packing tape to fill the gaps. Unfortunately it took pride of place in the garage sweatshop, so if you wanted to benefit from the cool air, you also had to work. A double-edged sword if ever there was one.

'You're fucking kidding me,' laughed David. I may have been full of polyester fluff, but David revealed that he had spent his childhood being called 'smurf boy' because of his blue hands and arms. Hunted down daily by the Vegemite gang, who had made his existence a living hell. David had grown up in a Footscray sweatshop that took up most of his family's tiny single-fronted house and garage. Their speciality was denim jeans. David was the youngest, and his arms were long and thin, so naturally his job was 'jean flipper'. Throughout his childhood, freshly sewn unwashed denim had permanently stained David's hands and arms blue. No amount of scrubbing would remove the blue dye.

His family worked well into the night, the hum of back-yard sweatshops like relentless cicadas all over the back lanes of Footscray. David fell asleep to the song of sewing machines and woke up to a mountain-high pile of jeans that needed flipping before he left for school. In the morning, his mother would rush him along, yelling, 'Jean first, after cartoon.'

So here we were, two first-generation Australians, former sweatshop kids, hiding in a damp Melbourne alleyway. University graduates with 'proper' jobs, sharing stories of childhood as I wolfed down one more cigarette in the rain. We had made it!

I have often wondered if they knew about us, the secret sweatshop kids. We knew about us; we existed all over the school playground. While some kids' clothes were covered in pet hair, we were covered in textile fluff or random threads. There was Vesna the Serbian, who grew up watching with envy as her mother sewed children's clothes, beautiful pink dresses with white gathered-lace trim, that they could never afford to buy at the shop. Vesna grew up with Nellie Oleson fantasies, while living the life of Laura Ingalls from St Albans. Sonia the Croatian brought a 2-metre black tent zip to school for show and tell one Monday morning. Our teacher was horrified at first as Sonia slowly pulled the zip out of the plastic bag like a tiger snake and proudly displayed it around her neck. Sonia loved to brag about the forts she made from the tents her mum sewed, and the camping trips, but we knew they were all bullshit stories. Maria the Greek grew up in piles of men's suits and always wore her thick black pigtails wrapped in ribbons made from the scraps of cheap shiny suit lining.

We were the kids who always had to rush home; work was always waiting for us. We never attended the birthday parties of our school friends, and ordering lunch from the canteen was a fantasy never to be attained; even today, the smell of greasy fast food takes me back to walking past the canteen and thinking, maybe tomorrow will be the day. We, the sweatshop kids, also knew never to tell our teachers why we were too tired to concentrate in class. In Grade 3, during reading time, my teacher yanked my pigtail so ferociously that she almost removed a chunk of my head. She must have thought this would help with my reading and concentration skills. After that, I made certain my first-generation immigrant arse learned to read, quick smart, and stay alert and awake.

My lungs are filled with tiny polyester fluffs. I don't know what the long-term effects are, and I'm too afraid to find out. Sometimes I imagine my lungs are white fluffy clouds or sweet sugary fairy floss, and this gives me a sense of calm.

Sibling

Hope Sneddon

Even before my brother died on Christmas morning, I hated the question *How many siblings do you have?*

The word sibling comes from Old English, where the term was originally used more generally to refer to kinship, relatives, or even friendship. These old meanings somehow encapsulate everything a brother or sister might be. They are kin and clan. You can see your ancestors' faces reflected back in you. They are relatives and relative to you. Your siblings come in order from oldest to youngest, and you're defined by where you fall in that line. The siblings next to you shape your personality, what you wear, how you speak, and your role in the house. They are linked to who you are, and it is through that relationality that you can find yourself. The distance between you and them becomes a touchstone for who you are together and apart. They are your first friends and your first enemies.

I grew up in Newcastle, the youngest of eleven children. People make their own conclusions about my family, and I am happier with their assumptions than I am with the truth. Let them think we're crazy Catholics or part of some cult. It's better than the reality. My mother had her first child at sixteen, and was married soon after. She would go on to have four more children before meeting my father. And he already had four children with his first wife.

When he and his wife separated, his four daughters lived in Sydney with their mother most of the time. I tell people that on meeting each other, and eventually marrying, my parents thought that nine kids weren't enough. So they had my brother and, six years later, me.

The term half-sibling originated in the twelfth century, where it was first used to describe siblings who have only one biological parent in common. It's not the same as a step-sibling, where you share no biological connection. On the contrary, with a half-sibling you share just enough biology for it to hurt that bit more.

I find it strange that it allegedly took humans so long to coin a term like half-sibling. It wasn't like the twelfth century was known for its immaculate family structures. The words created to describe the intricacies of life and families never cease to amaze me. These words have power, and not being privy to their meaning or application is a kind of shelter.

I only remember growing up with my brother, mother and father in our apricot-coloured housing commission home. My older siblings came and went. Mostly, they felt like strangers to me. Strangers I so desperately wanted to please, but never could. The intricacies of my parents' past and having nine other siblings old enough to have their own children my age didn't matter to me then. When you're young, you can't tell asbestos from marble or affection from an empty biscuit tin. Keith and I were stuck in the middle, somehow traversing familial fractals. We had half-siblings, were half-siblings. A half isn't a whole.

My brother Keith decapitated my favourite doll's head. I've broken his toe while we played soccer in our overgrown backyard.

He tackled me into a rose bush in our front yard. We both ended up covered in scratches and thorns. When I was six, I kept a small blue diary where I wrote about how much I hated him after we had a stupid fight. He read my diary and came to me crying. He asked me, 'Do you really hate me?' I told him, 'No, not really.' And we ripped the page out of the book together and burnt it in the backyard.

When I didn't understand what it meant to be 'the replacement family', my brother took my hand and we played Barbie and GI Joe until I forgot what I was asking him. We would walk to the corner shop, buy Ghost Drops and crush them between our teeth laughing at how the lollies stained our tongues. Then we would play Double Dragon for hours until the video game wiped our memories of all the screaming and fighting. We even made up an entirely new world – Teria – you just had to walk into our backyard behind the chicken coop, lift up the broken piece of wood, and enter.

We had each other, and we told each other this in the way we held hands. If we were just halves to our older siblings, it didn't matter, because together, we were whole.

As an adult, I lived many years abroad in Switzerland. My brother was always a call or message away, even though I was off finding myself in the bottom of a fondue pot. He often worked the night shift, and we messaged and talked like two old ladies throughout my day and his night. I used to help him stay awake, he would tell me. We were adults now, but still needed to find ways to hold each other. My brother and I talked endlessly about what it would be like for me to move back to Australia, and when

I surprised him with the news that I was moving to Melbourne at the end of 2019, I could hear relief in his voice.

I was supposed to start a new life in Melbourne. I was going to see my brother whenever I wanted and be there for his son's birthday parties. Keith and I talked a lot about it over Skype. All those sparkling new beginnings.

It wasn't long after returning to Australia that my brother called on a cold May morning to tell me he had cancer. Cholangiocarcinoma felt like a made-up word for a made-up reality in which neither he nor I belonged. Before we could understand how to pronounce his disease, Australia went into lockdown again, and the world was forced to learn a myriad of new realities and words unfamiliar. Covid reigned, and my brother's struggle felt so small. The world had changed forever, and there he was, dying of something so mundane as cancer. We were barred from each other's lives through relentless lockdowns and border closures. The short flight between Melbourne and Newcastle felt infinite and impossible.

I saw my brother for thirteen days, from when he was diagnosed with cancer to when he died, roughly six months later. I still don't know if thirteen is a lucky or unlucky number. I guess it depends on what side of the hospital bed you're on.

I emerged from the lockdowns with a missing piece. My brother was dead, and everyone else was celebrating Christmas and the new year. So many people were making up for lost time with hugs and pavlova while I sat at the Christmas table, swallowing cold turkey and the impossibly bitter taste of being grateful for my time with Keith.

At a recent dinner party, I was asked, 'How many siblings do you have?' And before I answered, I pondered the question. Was the answer ever ten? Is it nine now? Could it be one whole plus nine halves? Is that five and a half? Or is it four and a half now that Keith is gone? Is a sibling a sibling because they want to be one? Is it reciprocal – you're only siblings if you both agree? Do you have to grow up with them? Is a sibling still a sibling if they are dead? None of my answers seemed to fit, but then again, my family never fit into anything very well.

Fatty girl

Nina Wilton

I was in Year 3 the first time a boy asked me if my dad had ordered my mum in the mail. He grinned with the bravado of a child parroting something they weren't meant to overhear.

I had no way of understanding what the question meant, but I did understand it was something that cheapened them – cheapened us as a family – and I went hot with shame.

That evening, at our dinner table, I asked Dad what it meant. His outrage was immediate. It dropped loud and heavy among our plates and, unable to do anything with it, he blamed me for bringing it into our home.

Mum, desperate to understand, pulled at his sleeve.

He uttered a single, translated word and she shrank into herself.

Over time, I would grow used to Mum simmering in mortification, to the emotion churning deep down that she could never articulate well enough to bring to the surface. To her, this was more baseless gossip that othered her in a community of bored white, affluent women, and othered me in a school where you could count the non-white kids on one hand.

We had Paddle Pops and sweet sticky rice for dessert, and my parents never spoke of the incident with me again.

A year later, the same boy would make kissy faces at me and

coo with the others in exaggerated accents: 'Me so horny! Me love you long time!'

———

Mum didn't come to Australia as a mail-order bride; she came as an ESL student in love with an Australian boy she'd met in her village.

Her family were rice farmers deep in the jungle of Thailand's northern mountains, a place steeped in ancient superstition and nature, from which emerged stories of tigers prowling down dirt roads and ancestral spirits singing you lullabies while you slept. It was a place I'd later describe as very conservative, religious, but the true, traditional Thailand, where oxen still ploughed rice fields and Facebook was more pervasive than electricity.

It was in that village that twenty-year-old Mum, with her lightly freckled cheeks and ink-black hair past her hips, was in a motorbike accident with one of her brothers. She attended a pop-up clinic, with a cracked tooth, and was treated by a young, handsome dentistry student on overseas placement at the end of his degree. He was twenty-five and the youngest of a middle-class Catholic family in Sydney's East. She spoke no English, and he spoke a rudimentary Thai that was passable in the clinic, but really thrived in markets and bars. By the end of the consultation, Dad wanted to ask her out; Mum, wanting to seem more sophisticated, told him she was twenty-one.

Each time I recounted this story, instead of expected stories of trysts in red light districts and May to December romances in love motels, I was met with varying levels of surprise and bashfulness.

As a teen, I would confusedly receive questions about their age difference (five years), what attracted them to each other (probably the usual things), and even why Dad wanted an Asian woman (he didn't, he wanted my mum). It was as if by poking holes, people would uncover some perverted gap in this story that I must be concealing, something that explained why an eligible Australian boy would stumble across an Asian farm girl and move mountains to be with her.

———

Thai superstition dictates that you must never call a baby 'cute' or 'beautiful' for fear that malevolent spirits will want an attractive baby and come steal it. Accordingly, Thais will call and even nickname babies undesirable things: 'ugly', 'pig-nosed' – or, in my case, 'fat'. Ouan. Or pum pui. Fatty.

Mum was insistent, obstinate, despite hushed ridicule and the impression that she was some irrational babbling savage. Under her guard, I grew from a chubby baby into a cute little girl with a fringe and outfits resembling various fruits and flowers.

I grew again into a self-conscious, sweaty child, tormented by my flushed face and sweat stains on my school shirts. To hide those crescent-shaped stains, I would press my arms to my sides so tightly that I bruised myself. I would pinch the softness of my stomach and know deep within myself that I was undesirable.

In primary school, I was called the Asian Invasion, Ching Chong and, often, the Asian One. I spent afternoons on our tawny carpet amid dolls that were mostly blonde, the brunettes the closest approximation I could get to my own features. I watched

TV where the only relatable face was a timid sidekick, often of Japanese descent, often with a coloured streak in her hair, and almost always called Jade. In my attempts to fit what I saw as a mould for my personality, I felt aimless and wrong, like I was left standing in a game of musical chairs because I didn't understand the rules, or even why I was there in the first place. It felt natural, then, that my only option was to lean into my whiteness – it was meant to be half of me, after all.

I would force my eyes wide, determined that sheer willpower would stop them from looking slanty. I obsessively checked my eyelids in mirrors for fear of developing monolids, lamented the flatness of my facial profile, and slathered myself in coconut oil to tan my way to ethnic ambiguity.

I also discarded Mum with unrelenting cruelty, using hateful words and disgusted tones to make her smaller, hoping she'd disappear. I refused to recognise a word of Thai, demanded she speak English properly, and berated and tormented her for every misstep. I tried to sever whatever tied her to me, as if by pulling away from her I could rub the stain of her difference from my skin.

———

With time, my skin began to crawl with hormones that made me quick to snarl, that drew my voice high and filled my eyes with tears at the slightest confrontation. My developing frame was soft but shapeless and, in our beachside community, I felt repulsively childlike beside peers who were growing into curves. In my despair, an emboldened resentment arose. I dizzied in rage at Mum's attempts to help with Libra pads and hot water bottles, hurled boardshorts and rashies back in her face, and left uneaten the cut fruit she delivered to me.

I discovered that I'd also entered a new space of unrelenting assumptions. High school brought with it an unending downpour of comments about ping pong shows, happy ending massages and lady boys. Boys would gyrate and chant 'Bang-cock' at me, would grin and ask about the colour of my nipples, about whether all Thai women could fire objects from their vaginas, about whether my dad had picked up my mum in a topless bar.

I didn't have the vocabulary or insight to decipher my growing desire for whiteness, for being normal. I sought affection and validation from boys who were sometimes kind and always white. Some asked about my ethnicity or launched into a racial guessing game before asking my name, only to pointedly lose interest once establishing I wasn't an interesting kind of Asian. Others expressed opinions on Thai dishes, or dismissed me because they didn't like spicy food, or chuckled before telling me that Phuket was their favourite place in the world. Some said they didn't think of me as Asian, or that they didn't 'see' colour.

Slowly, I became hyper aware of these assumptions in my every breath and movement.

When I went with Dad to the shops, I would call him 'Dad' loudly or talk about what Mum was making for dinner, fearful that people thought we were dating, that in us they saw another dirty old white man with a young Asian girl. I started doing this at thirteen, and still I continue to do it, especially now that I wear a wedding band of my own.

I grew into my adult self not as a strong, wilful woman, but as a girl crippled by my sense of ugliness, a belief that my sexuality was not my own but dictated for me, like I was just a porn category. I was filled with mounting confusion about who I was. I had violently ripped out my heritage, only to realise that I would always walk the world as an Asian woman.

———

Once I reached university, I was able to taste invisibility, riding the bus into Sydney's inner west to a melting pot of a campus. I was surrounded by people from different ethnic backgrounds, different socioeconomic areas, with different facets to their identities, no longer one of a handful of Asian kids measuring my success through conformity.

But I also discovered that I occupied a space that was neither white nor Asian. While perceived physically as Asian, I was an outsider to groups of young people with immigrant parents who had grown up in an entirely different part of Sydney, who didn't speak the way I did, whose relationships with their parents, their language and culture was entirely different to mine. Often when meeting new people from other Asian backgrounds, they'd ask whether I spoke Thai, and when I said I didn't, they'd give me this condoling look and say, 'I'm sure your mum is sad about that.' To them, I was white.

While I was never called a 'banana' or a 'coconut', my connection to my physical self continued to mutate and devolve. I was a brown husk barely covering the shattered porcelain underneath. I was still tinged with an undesirability that I grew increasingly desperate to clean myself of.

I was once followed to my bus stop after a university play by a boy persisting with the racial guessing game. When I turned down his invitation for a drink, he asked if I had a boyfriend. At the time, I sort of did.

'Can I ask you a question?'

I bristled with suspicion but murmured, 'Yeah?'

'Is he white?'

I felt the eyes of everyone at the bus stop trail towards us. I was shivering from the wind, but heat rose in my face as I nodded.

He smirked. 'Good for you.'

It was like my paranoia and insecurities were as closely connected to me as my shadow. No matter where I went, they followed.

———

Eventually, I met the boy who'd become my husband in a friend's backyard over a Bunnings table and a pack of Winfield Reds. He had a barking laugh and big round eyes that had earned him the nickname Possum at work. He was easy to talk to, and when someone at the table stumbled for the words to ask me where I came from, he calmly corrected them: 'You mean, what's her background, right?'

And with him, I came to understand it was just that: background.

It formed part of the whole picture of me, but sat behind who I was as a person, behind my personality, behind my thoughts and feelings and needs. He was quick to provide the assurance and space for me to tend to myself and grow. I filled out the parts of me that I had emptied to make space for a false self, reacquainted myself with my face and body, and tiptoed into an abundance of culture that I'd always ignored. I spoke clearer and louder. I developed friendships founded in respect and understanding.

With time, I came to recognise the chasm I had created between myself and Mum. Slowly, painfully, I began to build a bridge to cross over and reacquaint myself with her. I came to see the village girl who fell off a motorbike, met a boy and crossed an ocean, having packed her bags full of dreams of being my mum. This girl scolded the white faces around her for calling me 'cute', welcoming alienation if that ensured my safety from hungry spirits.

So, whenever people make assumptions about what brought her here, I no longer feel shame but an immediate and unrelenting protectiveness.

Romance in Ramadan

Adrian Mouhajer

In the kitchen,
I watch Momma prepare kibbeh neyyeh
She drops a large glob of raw lamb into a metal bowl with a dull
    'thunk'
Pours a golden coil of rich olive oil from the long spout of a metal
    pourer
With her fists, she kneads the oiled pink mince – tender and
    malleable like the head of a newborn
Plunging her hands into the freezing cold water, ice cubes clinking
    together sharply,
She wiggles her fingers in the water, trying to stop the meat from
    sticking to her skin,
But traces of innocent flesh always remain.

When I was too young to fast from dawn till dusk,
I remember she'd let me lick the meat right off her fingertips,
I'd let her know if she'd added too much salt, or too little,
Nothing between us but love as I nibbled at her fingertips
Like a suckling lamb.

Now I can only watch her as hunger gnaws within me
She chops fresh coriander and minces garlic
Adds her special mix of nutmeg, cumin and black pepper
Before measuring out and pouring in the pomegranate molasses
With more care and precision than I've noticed in the past,
It's so viscous and glossy, I can almost see my reflection in the
    thick stream.
Afterwards, she washes her hands with soap and the silver from a
    spoon
to rid her hands of the smell of meat.

Her soapy hands grip the silver spoon,
Dark and wrinkled but strong and skilled,
I yearn for them to hold me, a desire buried within me that
    stretches across time
But I cannot go to her because she is as far away from me as the
    heavens are from the earth.
Though The Prophet (PBUH) said that Heaven lies beneath the
    feet of mothers
He never spoke of the children that have buried themselves at
    their mothers' feet.

As if she can read my thoughts,
my mother asks,
'So, is she coming tonight?'

We sit at the dinner table with the adhan crackling out of my
    parents' tower speaker,

Emergence

Always on, like a minaret in the sacred city,
For the full length of the holy month.

My father is seated at the head of the table, eyes closed
eyebrows gently furrowed in quiet contemplation waiting for the
   end of the adhan
so he can get up to pray Maghrib.

My mother sits on his left, her date already half gnawed,
she spits the seed on her plate and gulps some water.
She prefers her dates hard and chewy like I do
But I wish we agreed on more than just dates.

Ameera and I are sitting across from them
Her hands are in her lap beneath the table
And she is picking at the corner of her thumb.
I see crimson beginning to pool inside the torn skin,
I reach over and place my hand on hers.

My date is given a date; sticky, soft and sweet
As if she too has been fasting from dawn until dusk.
A newcomer to our table but an outsider to our faith
Yet we always honour our guests, as prophet Mohammed (SAW)
   reminds us
'… Let the believer in God and the Day of Judgement honour his
   guest.'

My mother piles Ameera's plate up high with kibbeh neyyeh and
      potato chips
My partner looks to me for reassurance, glancing up from behind
      her brown locks as if asking for permission,
I catch her eyes and smile, she breathes a sigh of relief and says:
'This looks amazing, kholto, but you've done too much!'
Kibbeh neyyeh, the stuff of hippie vegan nightmares
It's made of raw lamb and makes no attempt to appear otherwise,
Each province adds their own extra spice or style
But Mama's special blend of Syrian, Lebanese and Kuwaiti
      influence will always be my favourite.

I shift and wiggle in my seat, excited at Ameera finally getting this
      special peek into my childhood,
I watch her scoop the lamb onto a chip,
balancing it carefully,
bringing it to her lips.
She closes her eyes, savouring,
When she opens them, she is grinning unabashedly,
Like a child after their first big bite of birthday cake
'Wallah, kholto, the best kibbeh I've ever had. Better than my own
      teita's!'

That makes my mother smile, lips stretching wider than the gap
      between us
She looks at Ameera the way I wish she would look at me.
She lets her come over more than any other friends and thinks
      she's a 'good influence',

Emergence

But I could never be the good Lebanese girl Ameera is;
I'm more interested in bringing them home to meet my mother.

'You must give me the recipe! I need to make this for my family.'
Mama shakes her head, always possessive of her recipes
'When Nado gets married,' she nods at me 'then I can teach her.
Inshallah Allah will send her an ibn el halal one day
'...'
Ameera quietens at this, smile flickering as her eyes meet mine,
I smile in return; it's nothing I haven't heard before.
'Inshallah,' I say flatly.

I piece together a portion of kibbeh neyyeh for myself
Thinking I too have submitted my neck to the slaughter.

I dig my chip gently into the mince
Each bite coats my tongue with an intense, rich flavour
that's almost overwhelming
but the sourness of the pomegranate molasses cuts through the
    fattiness,
a sharp tang that brings me back to reality.

I lick my plate clean, scraping the pink off the white porcelain
    with my rough tongue,
Momma looks away without turning, like when we watch a movie
    together and she forgets about the kissing scenes,
Like last week when Ameera came over and emerged from my
    room glowing.

I am always hungry for more than Momma can provide,
and she can never bear to see me for who I am.

As I stare at the empty plate,
I find myself wishing we could share more than just food,
and that our conversations were as raw as this lamb.

I could use my tongue to further break my mother's heart.
'Momma, I want you to see Ameera as my future wife, not a
    future me.'

Instead, I swallow back the words with the last of the kibbeh
    neyyeh.
I won't get another taste of it until next Ramadan.
I utter my obligatory remarks
'Salam dayatik, Mama.'

Over tea and polite conversation
I accept that it is finally time for me to learn
how to make the dish myself.

For between my mother and I, there are some bridges that we
    cannot cross,
some sacrifices that cannot be made,
some places we can never venture together and
some meals we cannot share

No fish porridge for a metal ox

KT Major

Birth

'It's like taking a shit,' my grandmother once declared with relish. 'And out comes the baby.'

My waters break early. Families on both continents keep vigil by their phones. With borders shut, my parents from Singapore can't be here. Even my husband Peter's parents, who live minutes away, aren't allowed.

No one in my immediate family has ever had a natural birth.

My mother showed me the scars from her three caesareans. Jagged vertical lines where they cut the same spot open for me. Then again, for my younger sister.

My elder sister, Raine, suffered two stillbirths at eight months. Condolences flowed easily after the first. 'You'll try again, right?' Thick, uncomfortable silences after the second. Worse still was the brazen advice. 'Just adopt, *lah*,' Raine was told, still abed in hospital, her insides wrecked. We cremated the tiniest of caskets on her behalf.

The pall of past tragedy looms while my organs contort in the agony of labour. Eighteen hours in, the blessed anaesthetist arrives. After two more hours of pushing, my obstetrician says I need help. Being stuck for so long, my baby's heart rate has dipped dangerously. I don't hesitate. With the aid of an episiotomy and forceps, they place a bawling, bloody baby on my chest.

He stops crying when he hears our voices, warm and familiar. We've spoken to him every day about our hopes, dreams and love. I'll never forget his look of dawning recognition: wide eyed and curious about the people he just met but knows so well.

We ring our parents. One hour old, our son attends his first video call. Peter's parents crack open some wine. Pa sheds tears of joy. Our son shares the same birthday as Raine, on Singapore's National Day.

Then my son takes a shit on me. 'A fresh gown, please?' I burble groggily. The nurse obliges. While Peter cuddles our newborn, I pass out, my front in a clean gown, my back still in a pool of blood and gore.

Name

My poetic father gave us poignant and unusual Chinese names. My name means 'all-rounded' yet 'humble'. Such is his talent that our extended family turns to him for baby names. '*Aiyoh*,' he once lamented. 'So much pressure.' And yet he delivers. In time, Raine has a son who receives a beautiful name as well.

For my son JM, Pa chose the character 'Jie', meaning 'outstanding'. When I announce this to Peter's Aussie family, they try to pronounce the crisp 'Jie' sound, which requires touching your tongue to the back of your top teeth. They practise diligently but mostly make thick and gummy 'J's, like in 'jam'. I suggest trying a 'Z' sound, and they switch to buzzing like bees. 'Oh well,' says Peter. 'He can always change it to "Jim".'

Mostly, I whisper 'Jie, mei shi' (It's okay) to soothe him: after jabs, bellyaches, head bumps, or when he wants cuddles. What I say to him as a child will become his inner voice. I want him to find comfort in his Chinese name, chosen reverently by his doting grandfather. Plenty of schoolyard teasing to come. Or he may grow to hate it and change it to 'Jim'. Until then, I hope he'll remember the love and poetry in his name. I also reserve the right to yell it like a fishwife when annoyed.

Feed

We swore black and blue not to do traditional 'confinement'. No antiquated taboos, like not being allowed to wash my hair. We wanted time alone as a new family, not constant visitors.

Strangely enough, the pandemic fulfils our wish. With a newborn in lockdown, we tough it out alone for eight weeks. Peter's parents wear masks in the driveway to meet JM for the first time.

Not knowing when she might meet JM, Ma ramps up her regime of grandparenting through WhatsApp. 'Consider these confinement foods,' reads a long text. 'Pork in dark vinegar. Boiled barley water. Stewed black chicken with red dates.'

'Where to find these in lockdown, Ma?' I text back furiously. 'I'm not bloody cooking.' Thanks to JM injuring my coccyx, sitting is pure agony.

'Should've sourced beforehand,' Ma replies. Closing WhatsApp in fury, I order hot chips from Uber Eats and eat standing up.

When JM is ten months old and my parents are finally able to visit, I psych myself for a real fight, expecting years of pent-up advice on raising children. Especially feeding.

Growing up in Singapore, I drank cow's milk formula, like most babies. Without shame, too. But here, the pressure to breastfeed is immense. Even though I was physically unable to produce enough milk, I still felt guilty giving up after trying and suffering for months.

I was weaned on fish porridge made with rice, mackerel and – shock, horror – soy sauce or sugar. No allergens – like eggs, sesame and nuts – until much later.

The advice today is different. I feed JM a variety of purees, finger foods and most allergens by twelve months old, to avoid him developing allergies later.

JM starts solids at five months, consuming roughly a full cup per meal. I struggle to keep up: with the sheer volume of cooking, ensuring nutrition and variety, and introducing allergens. I curse at having to introduce tree nuts individually, through expensive nut butters or sweating over a mortar and pestle. And we still need a pantry full of store-bought baby food to supplement my cooking.

When they arrive for their visit, Ma immediately inspects the Airbnb's kitchen. Next morning, she says casually, 'Come for lunch. I made fish porridge.'

'JM won't eat it,' I reply serenely.

'Why not?' Her voice is dangerously calm.

'He likes variety.' Telling Ma he dislikes rice would be akin to a blood betrayal.

Emergence

At lunch, Ma serves my favourite chicken wings, managing to deep-fry them in the smallest of saucepans. As expected, JM refuses the porridge. Ma promptly assumes her food is not tasty and is only mollified when the adults lick their plates clean.

That evening, I show her JM's dinner – egg frittata with vegetables, hummus, kale, bok choy and lamb mince. A mini almond muffin and fruit for dessert. He finishes everything.

Ma sees our freezer full of homemade baby food, the specially baked muffins, and how JM feeds himself (messily) and drinks from an open cup. Her face is wistful. I still remember her running after my baby sister Brie with a spoonful of fish porridge, begging and cajoling. I hope for a whiff of praise, perhaps, for our effort in feeding JM.

Ma clears her throat. 'No wonder he won't eat my fish porridge.' And she never mentions the porridge again. I take that as a win.

Sleep

'One more word and I'm packing up and going home!' I roar at my parents.

On holiday with my visiting family on the New South Wales South Coast, trouble has struck. The bedroom we wanted for JM is basically an oven, and the centrally controlled AC refuses to work. So we put JM's cot downstairs in the lounge. By himself.

Ma and Pa are furious. 'Why are you abandoning him?'

My sister Brie stays silent. She knows how torturous it was from her last visit when JM was four months old.

JM slept with us for the first four months, but his colic and sleep regression woke us all at least six times a night. Day naps lasted only twenty minutes – barely time to eat, shower, feel human again. I expressed breastmilk while he napped, praying the pump would go faster so I could use the bathroom. I felt like my skull had been chiselled open – my thoughts splintered and consciousness fractured. Muscles moved without control, like that damn AC. Peter struggled to work while I flailed under the torrent of laundry and cleaning.

Broken, we were referred to Figtree Hospital's residential sleep clinic. Their nurses and doctors saved us. They figured out how to settle JM, who, unsurprisingly, only responded to a very specific routine. We'd been doing it all wrong.

At Figtree, I had my first panic attack. After JM's birth, we had had two harrowing ER visits, first for excruciating mastitis and then for his severe colic. That evening at Figtree, JM woke up crying inconsolably. I froze, thinking in horror, 'Not the hospital again,' completely forgetting we were already in a hospital and help was only a push-button away.

The kind nurse Juliette let me have a good cry and bundled me into another room to sleep – my first eight-hour stretch in ages.

I was later able to seek therapy.

When we got home, Peter and I took turns sleeping in the same room as JM, so the other could rest. After six months of persevering with the routine, JM now prefers to sleep on his own, often till morning. I'm forever grateful I'm able to access help like this in Australia.

My parents haven't seen any of this. Sleep training is alien to many Asian cultures; fussy babies are part of parenthood for years.

Back at the holiday house, Pa is persistent. 'Can't he sleep in your room?'

'End of discussion, or I'm going home!' I explode. They sigh loudly. Ignoring them, I scrub bottles more vigorously than needed. Peter puts JM to bed.

After a while, Brie pokes her head around the door. 'Want to play cards?'

Pa shuffles in. 'Is he asleep?' I show him the baby monitor. JM is fast asleep, the temperature perfect. Pa marvels at the video, sound and temperature sensors, technology he never had. Ma recalls finally evicting us from her bedroom – when we were five. We break out the cards for Dai Dee, an Asian card game. Peter wins almost as often as Ma.

Play

Born in the year of the Metal Ox, JM is headstrong and boisterous. After kicking relentlessly in utero, he tried to climb Peter's shoulder while being burped – the day he was born.

We start tummy time at six days old. Months later, when he is visibly frustrated at being unable to crawl, I move toys away just as he reaches for them. He propels himself forward like an indignant seal.

Many comments from my family on his videos: 'Playground bully!' and 'Tiger Mum!'

I adore finding ways to amuse my son: silly songs, peek-a-boo, puzzles and books. But he also gets to play independently in his playpen, under close watch.

More comments: 'He needs cushions!' JM's playpen is safe and padded, a luxury I never had.

JM has barely learned to crawl before he wants to walk. And run. Undeterred whether he falls on his bum or face, he needs hours of stimulation. Peter's parents find it tricky to change JM because he writhes like a muscly worm, and kicks your groin like an ox.

Expecting more comments when they visit, I am surprised by Ma. I watch as she holds JM expertly while he attempts forty bounce squats. Knowing his love of words ending with 'oo', Ma says '*Diu qiu!*' in Chinese as she plays ball with an ecstatic JM.

From her forty years of teaching, Ma somehow morphs into all of the Wiggles, and can sing and play for hours, especially with my nephew Zed. On cue, Raine and Zed ring us, woeful that they can't be there to play.

I'm surprised, not only by the dial-up in Ma's energy when playing, but at the contrast from all other times. Stuck at home in a pandemic, my parents have grown frail. Pa's face is pinched, and he now needs a cane, while Ma likes to maintain appearances with a sturdy umbrella.

The most painful part of their visit isn't the fighting. It's witnessing how old and fragile they've become, how their steps falter, and appetites have shrunk.

Tossing another ball to JM, Ma says: 'Why don't you rest? I got him. JM knows you're nearby. Children are always okay when they know their parents are near.'

I lie back on the sofa gratefully, my eyes wet. We've waited so long for this.

Mah jong instructions for life

Vanessa Yenson

Ask Mum or Dad how to choose the seating order.

You need a pile of the four winds, each player picks one; this reminds you of the start of Scrabble, another family favourite, but a game in which you rarely win. East chooses their seat and the other winds sit in their relative position – luck is a large part of mah jong. If you are East, choose wisely – there is always one seat that picks up the dud tiles. *In your family, you are the youngest of four. Through different times of your life this may have seemed lucky or unlucky, but you did not choose the birth order and you did not choose your fate.*

Shuffle the tiles facedown on a felt mah jong table; your favourite is the one made by Uncle David with little wooden drawers to store your gambling money. He is not related, but all elders are referred to as aunty and uncle. Shuffling is noisy, even on the green felt – the smooth tiles clatter beneath your fingers. *Don't shuffle like your grandmother (Por-Por), who moved the tiles back and forth under her hands without letting them mingle with the rest. Everyone liked to play against Por-Por because she lost with regular enthusiasm.*

Each player assembles a two-storey wall of seventeen tiles and pushes it forwards at an upward angle to form a rhombus with overlapping edges. It was harder with little hands but, as you grew, you learned to brace the wall with outstretched fingers, using each pinkie as an anchor at either end. According to the internet, the corners need to touch so there are no gaps for evil spirits to enter. *You must have left a gap in one of the games in your childhood – the evil spirits biding their time until you were an adult.*

Ask Mum or Dad how to choose who starts as banker. The wind of the first round is East – you need to roll the dice; this has nothing to do with the seat you chose, which was also determined by the East wind. You might be confused at this point, but Mum and Dad know best, so just follow their lead. *Mum and Dad brought the family to Sydney when you were a toddler and they still lead the way decades on; their steady example has guided you through the most difficult periods of your life.*

The role of banker sticks if they win the game; if they lose, the role moves anticlockwise. If you win as banker, everyone pays you double. If the winning hand includes the wind of the round or another high value card (such as a dragon), they get paid double. If the banker collects the wind of the round and wins, they get double again. Some people win and win again through life. *For a time, you were not one of them.*

Once the bank comes back to the start, the wind of the round changes. East. South. West. North. *Your grandparents were from the East. They migrated from a poor farming village in rural China to South Africa. Escaping communism and landing in apartheid, where they didn't fit in as white or black.*

The banker throws the dice – they tumble over each other in their randomness within the rhombus, bouncing on the felt and off the tiles. Chance upon chance upon chance. Luck determined your seat, the shuffle of the tiles, the role of banker, the roll of the dice and the start of the game. Mah jong dice have black dots, except for the numbers one and four, which are red. Red is a lucky colour in Chinese culture. Red is the colour of blood. *Your blood, it turns out, was not so lucky.*

Count clockwise, starting with the banker, stopping at the player determined by the dice roll. If the banker rolls a five, their wall is broken at the fifth tile. Players collect their hand – two pairs at a time – from the sixth tile onwards, starting with the banker. Once each player has twelve tiles, the banker 'jumps' – taking the first top tile, skipping one and picking up the next. The banker starts with fourteen tiles. Each subsequent player takes one extra to start with thirteen. *Life is not an equal playing field.*

Open your hand to face you, again like Scrabble, but these tiles are sturdier and able to stand independently. Align the matching suits, like in a game of gin rummy, put the numbered tiles in order and group the disconnected (rubbish) tiles to the side of your hand. You might need to consult the handwritten cheat sheet of Chinese characters (*hanzi*) in the mah jong case. *Even now, you are unable to isolate one number of Cantonese in your head without running through all ten – echoing wasted Sunday classes as a four-year-old when you learned a language that your parents couldn't speak. Before you moved to Australia, Por-Por was your favourite. You toddled after her around the garden in Essexwold, Johannesburg, while your siblings climbed the mulberry tree or attended school to learn Afrikaans. Your two-year-old mind understood the dialect she spoke, languages being so malleable for children; but then you had to leave her behind, her significance and any connection to language dulled over time.*

The green dragon reminds you of a cabbage, and you only recently realised that if you turn the tile the right-way up, it is actually an intricate formation of *hanzi. Your connection to your ancestral land faded with each migration, until Por-Por was just a solemn face in a sepia photograph staring at you from the past.*

The banker starts by discarding one tile, placing it upright in the middle of the table. This is usually a rubbish tile, like an unimportant wind, or ones and nines. Any player can '*poong*' this tile off the table for three of a kind, however only the next player can '*soong*' to make a run – either of which needs to be claimed aloud before play continues. As *soong* can only be 'fed' by the person before; players lament (often loudly) if they are 'hungry'. As a child, you often heard the aunties cry out 'feed me!' while you hid under the tables in games of hide-and-seek with your cousins. *As an adult, Mum prepared homecooked meals when you could no longer stomach the bland hospital fare. Chemotherapy made your gag reflex so sensitive that the sight of the pink trays with their pink cloches made you dry retch. You might still react this way at the mention of them.*

The claimed *poong* or *soong* is displayed upright in front of the player's concealed hand as a reminder of what tiles are no longer in play, and a potential gauge of the hand that is being collected. *You could not conceal your status in the world. Your bald head incompletely hidden beneath a beret drew stares from strangers in Westfields and parishioners in church alike. You tried not to read into expressions, too fatigued to carry others' pity on top of your own physical and emotional trauma.*

Each player takes their turn, moving anticlockwise. When you take a tile from the wall, you must sigh in disgust – uttering the South African phrase 'Ag, no man!' is optional, but effective. It is also optional to fiddle with this tile as you contemplate your options. You might want to ask Mum or Dad for help. *Mum and Dad were always there to help you – Dad visited before and after work, and Mum slept nights on a fold-out camping bed in your hospital room, going home during the day to shower and cook. They shadowed you on dinners to Leichhardt, ready to shepherd you home when you couldn't keep up with your friends. You did not like to ask for help. You were fierce in your independence, but you reverted into the little girl needing her mummy during the darkest moments after diagnosis, and then after relapse.*

Luck and chance might start the game, but you need strategy to win. Always go with the tactic that gives you the most options – if you have a one, three and four, it would be prudent to discard the one rather than the four, so you have two options to complete your run. Waiting for middle pips should be avoided where possible, which is why ones and nines can often be considered rubbish tiles. *There was strategy when you relapsed, but it was limited to just one option – you needed a bone marrow transplant. The search for a compatible donor commenced as you went back in for more chemo.*

When a player is waiting for one tile to win, they are 'calling'. This is met by murmurs from the other players, speculating what they are calling for. You look at their *poongs* and *soongs*, think back to the tiles they had previously discarded and try to piece together any patterns. You might need to change up your collections to block their win. Calling requires patience. *You were never very patient in life, wanting to grow up quickly and join in with your siblings. You hated being the youngest – smaller, slower, weaker. 'Calling' for a bone marrow donor was an agonising wait.*

The red dragon is shaped like a vertical sword, its lines etched in deep like scars of dried blood ending in a point. There are four red dragons in the mah jong set. Four identical swords steeped in blood. Blood is produced by stem cells in the bone marrow. *Your siblings' bone marrows were identical, but yours was not.*

The white dragon looks like a mirror with blue parallel lines superficial to the touch. *Some similarities with your siblings were skin deep, and yet genetic ties stretched back over countries and language and culture and time. None of them could be your bone marrow donor, but those two years strengthened the invisible threads of your shared experience, intertwining your stories in a unique and enduring way.*

———

It might seem that mah jong focuses on strategy and winning, where players employ rules and tactics to outfox opponents, so they can leave with the heaviest pockets. There can be much glee in pulling off a high-stakes win, but it is not the money that draws us together.

Today, our connectedness surfaces when we sit around Uncle David's handmade table on Christmas afternoons, when bellies are full and conversations flow. When my nieces and nephews hear tales about Por-Por, of the struggles and joys of life in Johannesburg, and anecdotes from our own childhood. The interweaving of our individual threads grows thicker with each generation, each story, and each shuffle of the mah jong tiles.

How do you say yes to a kiss that will change you?

Zoë Amanda Wilson

She said, 'I want to kiss you, but I don't think this is the appropriate venue.'

I paused. That pause contained everything that had happened in my life in the past not-quite thirty-one years. The safe predictability of sex and romance with men. The reasonable proxy for love that I felt for them. The identity that had been handed to me, raised in Canberra by unremarkably conservative parents and Catholic schools – the same identity that I had obediently donned in the same way that I had passively accepted offers of companionship from men throughout my adult years.

But now I had to make a choice.

'I want to kiss you …'

The pause also contained everything that would happen to me from that point onwards. This might change my life. I tried to look into the future and understand what it might mean for me to kiss this woman, but I couldn't focus on anything but her, so real there in front of me. No attempt to hide her raw desire, deriving great amusement from the effect this was having on me. I was convinced she could hear the roaring in my ears and the racing of my brain. She could certainly see my lips shaking and my shallow breathing; there was no way to conceal that. A mixture of terror and desire fought to guide my response to her statement as it hung between us.

In the end, it was pragmatic curiosity that won out, as usual. I had only begun swiping women on Tinder, just to see how other women presented themselves on the app. I had only swiped her to see if she might swipe me back. I had only accepted her offer of dinner to see what it would be like to go on a date with a woman. As it turned out, it was rather similar to dates with men, on the surface.

We ate Mexican and chatted about movies and travel. I learned she was an only child, and her dad was Egyptian. She had studied literature at uni, and she loved cats. But in all of the important ways, it was entirely different to any other date. I wore my sexiest outfit and spent the whole night sitting on my hands and trying to remind myself to breathe. I was desperate to impress her and also felt completely incapable of doing so. At any given moment, I was either breathlessly babbling, or silently transfixed by her face. Her mouth and her eyes. She was perfectly relaxed; a consummate maven at making women uncomfortable.

I was only there to see what it would be like to go on a date with a woman, and the answer was ... it was deeply destabilising. And now I had the opportunity to see what it would feel like to kiss her.

I said, 'What is the appropriate venue?'

She smiled and suggested her car, parked a couple of blocks away. She led the way, almost dancing in front of me with palpable glee. I walked stiffly behind her, my arms wrapped around me – protection against the frigid air and my own creeping doubts. She wanted to kiss me. I knew that this would change my life. I could not kiss this woman then go back to pretending I was what I had always been. Suddenly it all seemed very inconvenient, and indeed almost unfair for her to suggest it. She shouldn't be allowed to go around shaking the very bedrock of people's existence on otherwise unexceptional cold Thursday evenings in autumn.

I sighed and mentally stepped back from the precipice on which I had been teetering. I wasn't ready for this. I might never be ready. And that was okay. I was happy and I was fine. I didn't see any driving urge to plunge myself into an uncertain situation just to explore something that I had never really suffered the lack of. I began preparing myself to let her down. When we arrived at her car, she would ask me again if she could kiss me, and I would decline, as gracefully as I could. I would apologise for wasting her time, and thank her for the Mexican. I would go home and switch my Tinder preferences back to men only, satisfied that I had tried dating women and it just wasn't for me.

And then I would go to bed and dream about her.

———

She opened the driver's side door and ushered me in, cranking the heater to warm me while she quickly cleared the passenger seat of basketballs and bags of clothes – evidence of a partially completed house move. I was waiting for the right moment to explain I had changed my mind about the whole kissing thing.

83

And then she kissed me.

And I changed.

I sat rigidly while she gently grabbed my face in her hands and put her lips on mine. Every single atom in my body blasted apart from one another, then came back together again in an instant – so different to how they had been before. Time and space existed only in that moment, in that car, in the space between our bodies. Her hands moved down my neck and to my waist. Her tongue found mine. I kept my eyes open to convince myself that she was real. I had never seen anything so beautiful. I had never felt anything so soft. I had never smelled anything so coconutty.

She finally pulled away.

'You can touch me, you know.'

Could I? I couldn't quite fathom it. My body was locked. I retrieved my hand from underneath my legs, where it had found itself again. I contemplated stretching it out towards her and touching her. I looked at her face, her neck, her waist. The thought of touching her there evoked another violent wave of adrenalin, so I attempted something that seemed more manageable. I circled my fingers around her wrist. I was awestruck by its perfection. I turned it over in my hands, marvelling over its softness, its daintiness, its vulnerability. Somehow that tiny, exquisite body part represented everything that was perfect about this woman, about all women. And suddenly I was in love with her.

———

That's all that mattered for a while. I was gay now, but I barely noticed. My sexuality was entirely a function of my relationship with her. It hadn't struck me yet that I was now part of a minority group, a community in which I would have difficulty finding my footing – newly out, femme-presenting lesbians are not very high on the queer hierarchy. None of that mattered, only her. Every aspect of her was so novel to me that it appeared the very perfect version of itself, the archetypal exemplar of its category.

I found new dimensions of myself as well. Until now I had existed only as the girl-half of conventional heterosexual relationships; I had never experienced the delight of moving gracefully between traditionally masculine and feminine roles. She and I performed a constant delicate pas de deux of command and surrender, strength and softness. She opened doors for me; I carried the heavy groceries. I built her IKEA furniture while she cooked me dinner. I felt myself expanding into a fuller, truer version of the woman I was always meant to be. She was perfect, and I was perfect when I was with her.

She's not around anymore. I mean, I suppose she does exist somewhere out in the world, re-watching *Seinfeld* and drinking negronis and biting her nails. I probably still follow her on Instagram or something. But the version of her that I created, that flawless ideal that I worshipped in my mind, began to crumble the moment that she sat me down that night, nine months and seventeen days after the kiss, and told me that she probably didn't love me.

I resented her for a while. I am gay, and now it matters. She taught me what real love feels like – the kind of love that has historically created art and started wars and caused revolutions. But now I have no idea what to do with it. I am gay and heartbroken and alone, and it isn't fair. But as I work at dismantling the idol I created of her in my mind, through which is inextricably woven all of the things I learned through her, I notice that it isn't leaving the hole I thought it would. The raw materials I used to construct it remain, and they are mine. The vast, fierce, fathomless love that I have unlocked, and the new understanding about what it means to be fully, authentically myself in the world, knowing that my identity is one that I alone created.

It was never really her who changed me. She just had to be there for it to happen.

Ancestor memory

Raelee Lancaster

One

It's the start of a new decade: the 1970s. Bell-bottoms and disco are all the rage, and my Aunty B and Uncle G are at Gulargambone Aboriginal Reserve. Aunty is fresh faced, dark haired, and wears a white dress with long sleeves and a hem that hits her mid-thigh. Next to her, Uncle stands tall – the tallest I've ever seen him. His short curls sit close to his head, and he wears a dark shirt with pale flowers. They each have a child on one of their hips. Another child stands in front of the two of them, holding Uncle's hand. The family look at the camera controlled by a visiting journalist. Aunty B has the hint of a smile, while the rest of the family wear more stoic expressions. In this same year, seven of her children – including the three being photographed now – will be taken by government officials.

Far from Gulargambone – and even further from the political agenda of the 1970s, an agenda that preached self-determination while stealing children – I study this image in an archive as a student of world history. It's funny: having the world at your fingertips and the only thing you can imagine is home. There is a weight in my chest as I sit in this archive. The grief of having Elders pass into the Dreaming at alarming rates. The anxiety of not quite having enough of the jigsaw to piece our histories together. The heaviness of understanding what my family has survived.

In the poem 'Her Memory Remember', Natalie Harkin (2019) writes, 'colonial-archive remember / oral-history remember … my grandmother remembering / her memory I remember'. It is this poem I return to as I work with and move through archival institutions. The past is very present here. The version of Aunty B I know is a grey-haired grandmother to me, sister to the paternal grandmother I never knew. I have a recent image of her saved on my mobile phone. Aunty B is hugging Uncle G's face tightly to her chest. She has lines at the corners of her mouth and eyes – kind eyes that shine with the kind of love Frank O'Hara writes about in that Coke poem. Next to her, Uncle G is in a hospital bed. His eyes are closed but he is awake, sending the camera a gum-filled grin. Only a few strands of hair remain on his head and his flesh is wrinkled tissue paper.

But I know this dark-haired version of Aunty B, too. The way she says *I love you* with actions more than words. The way she hugs me too tight, afraid to say goodbye. I notice myself mirroring her the older I become. As if I'm acting on muscle memory.

Mine.

And hers.

These memories are my inheritance. They shape the woman I am, the woman I will be. They live in my DNA – more vivid and more permanent than any photograph.

Two

It's 2016, and the A History of the World in 100 Objects exhibition features at the National Museum of Australia. A group of friends and I make the trip to Canberra in the spring. This was not our first long-distance trip to see a touring show. The four of us met four years prior in the place where most lifelong friendships are made: the theatre. Our shared love of history, drama and wearing black in summer meant we often frequented arts and cultural institutions, about once a week.

This trip, however, feels different. It is my last with the group before I leave the rat race of Sydney for the wet heat of Brisbane. The air is full of nostalgia and excitement. M drives, and we joke about how bonkers she must be to still own a car in Sydney. Where M's car is small and low, M is over six feet tall with a Slenderman body and the bone structure of a *Deep Space Nine*–era Terry Farrell. I sit in the front passenger seat and look on in awe as I watch her fold herself into the vehicle. C and J take too many photos. Before they hop in the backseat, they capture an image of me in an orange and black dress with an Ancient-Greek pottery design. I preen like a cat as they tell me I'm beautiful, even though my hair is still wet from my early morning shower. C adds each image to a fresh folder in her phone's picture gallery. For posterity, C says. She tells us that if we document anything on the trip, we must take note of the date and location. She's a true student of history.

We sing along to the *Hamilton* soundtrack for the length of the trip. We talk about history – how the so-called 'Founding Fathers' would have hated rap and how people of colour reclaiming white-washed stories is exactly the material we need to be consuming.

Emergence

I note the lack of Native American voices in the musical and feel the excitement and nostalgia turn to a hovering grey cloud. When in doubt, mentioning colonial violence is sure to quiet a room.

Too soon, we arrive at the museum. The foyer is bright, boisterous and open. We enter the exhibition and encounter an enclosed, quiet and dimly lit space. The air is cold and tastes sweet and musky. My feet immediately lead me to a narrow case displaying a long russet pandanus-fibre basket. I eye the pale plaque at the bottom left of the case. The small black text acknowledges the millennia of cultural knowledge imbued within that one object. I wonder if that acknowledgement goes any deeper. If the museum has even let the community know their ancestral information is on display in an international exhibition. If the acknowledgement is part of the original plaque copy, circulating to other Commonwealth countries. Or if it is a late, Australian-only addition that allows the curators to pat themselves on the back as they trip over that exceedingly low bar.

I read the other information stated on the plaque. I memorise the museum number developed by non-Aboriginal cataloguers for their western identification purposes. I read the full name of the white man who once owned the item. Finally, the creator of the basket: an unnamed and unknown 'Aboriginal Australian'. My friends mention how great it is that the museum has included Aboriginal culture in the exhibition. I love them dearly – they are the closest thing to family I have in Sydney – but at that moment, I need to take a moment for myself.

When my feet can drag my body forward, I see missing information scattered throughout the exhibition. Peoples unnamed, provenances unknown. Colonial history is written to erase whatever came before it. The wealthy European gaze is situated as the norm and the white man is the neutral, unbiased observer. Land stolen, repurposed, renamed. People stolen, repurposed, unnamed. As if we could ever forget. As if each one of us isn't an archive of ancient knowledge.

Jazz Money (2020) calls Indigenous people 'gifted data managers' who create 'within a cultural landscape imbued with legacy, responsibility, and sacred or ancient skills'. Where westerners may see an unalive and unassuming artefact, we see living culture and kinship. Standing here at the National Museum of Australia, I don't see a basket. I see my fingertips stained by dyed raffia as my Aunties teach me what their aunties taught them. I smell the fresh dirt of Wiradjuri, Wailwan and Kamilaroi Countries, where my feet feel freest. I hear the yarns spun by the world's oldest living orators.

This basket is not just a basket.

It is raw data.

It is continuous survival.

It is memory.

Three

It's 2001, and I sit in the front row of the school assembly hall in my maroon-and-blue school uniform, sporting my two new front teeth. My dad and uncles are on the stage before us: skinny black legs, red laplaps, and white ochre splashed across their fronts. I watch wide-eyed as my peers are called to the stage to partake in the dance the men are teaching. I feel incredibly smug seeing my family embody each new animal, knowing each call from the yidaki before anyone else.

My dad calls for volunteers between each dance. Uncle R sends me cheeky grins from the stage. He sits, crouched, and waves his hand at me, silently telling me to come up. On the last dance, I raise my hand. Dad's eyes glance over me, and he picks one of the boys sitting in the Year Two row behind. I'm furious. His own daughter!

I keep my hand up as Dad continues his search. Kangaroos. Hunters. Emu. There's a fire in my belly. *Who's gonna be the tree now?* he asks his captivated audience. Icy water quenches my fire when he calls me up to the stage.

Twenty years and that memory still plays in my mind. The way my peers snicker as I walk up on that stage. The way I hold my hands up in the air like branches, glaring at Dad as he dances around me. The way I don't speak to him for two weeks after this day.

The kangaroo, the emu, the trees – they're all connected, he says as he plaits my hair before bed. *We show them all the same respect.* He says this to teach me values that link all Aboriginal people. Lessons of respect and reciprocity. While I am not his blood – him, a proud Kamilaroi man, and me, a small Wiradjuri girl – he teaches me all he can. He teaches me on land that is not ancestral home for either of us, land we have migrated to and care for as much as we are able.

The intersection of this place and time is where my memory feels the crispest. Days sitting by the lake, trying to catch fish with a single blue-plastic coil of fishing line and homemade bait.

Throw the line there, where the water looks darker. Did you see that air bubble? Right there. Those afternoons walking through the bush with only a stick. *Take a couple of leaves and spit into your hands. That's it. Now rub your hands together really fast. See the suds? That's bush soap, bub!*

In a text produced for an online exhibition, Nathan Sentance writes, 'ngurang (place – Wiradjuri language) teaches you. It provides knowledge through experience … Ngurang allows us to transverse time, giving us immediate connection to our ancestors'. As I grow, I see memories like this with a new lens. Where my arboreal acting debut was once coloured in shame, it is now a frank lesson in kinship and humility.

Some memories are only now resurfacing as if, years ago, they cocooned themselves high in the canopies of my mind, waiting for the right time to emerge. As these memories flourish, I remember who we were before my pre-teen arrogance swept in and Dad's days blurred into dizzying highs that pulled him further and further away from us. In his exhibition piece, Sentance goes on to say, 'As a Wiradjuri man, I have river in my blood, I have wind in my bones, and the sound of birds in my voice.' This is a familiar experience that I and many other Blackfullas know. I hold these memories wherever I go.

I am my dad.

I am that basket.

I am my Aunty B.

I am my ancestors' memory.

References

Harkin, N., 'Her Memory Remember', in *Archival Poetics 3: Blood Memory*, 2nd ed., Vagabond Press, 2019, p. 10.

Money, J., 'Sacred data', Museum of Contemporary Art, https://www.mca.com.au/stories-and-ideas/sacred-data/, 26 May 2020.

Sentance, N. & Lancaster, R., 'Ngurang-dhi – from place', EX-EMBASSY Exhibition and Text Series, https://ex-embassy.com/en/commissioned-texts/nathan-sentance-raelee-lancaster/, 2018.

I have a lot to learn from my mother

Helen Nguyen

Climbing barefoot onto Ong Ngoai and Ba Ngoai's grave, Mum lets her slippers fall. They plonk onto the white pebbles, her bark-coloured coat draping over the granite tombstone. The wind whispers through Fawkner Cemetery. Mum kneels down and begins gently wiping the headstone. Her jade bangle glints like mould in the overcast light. Her rectangular face is smooth as a lychee jelly cup, skin pearly and plump from laser appointments. Dad stands behind her in his Kathmandu puffer jacket. He carefully places pink lady apples, oranges and mandarins in a pyramid shape on a plate. After turning fifty, Dad's hair thinned and is now a battle of silver and black across his moon-shaped scalp. Mum sits him down with a box of Coles-bought L'oréal 'natural black' hair dye every month.

If I were any younger, I would have rolled my eyes and complained at the unfairness of spending my Sunday morning at the cemetery. Dead people can't eat. But this time, I am trimming the stems of water lilies, carefully arranging them with the gypsophila in the grave vase. I have a lot to learn from my mother.

Emergence

'My mum is stupid,' I declared loudly for the lanky, acne-faced boys in white Tommy Hilfiger T-shirts. It was a chilly September night in East Melbourne and Ed Sheeran songs were pumping from Pat O'Brian's tennis court. Disco lights flickered candy-like on his aqua-illuminated pool. My mother had written a note to give to Pat's parents at the entrance because I was under-aged, a smart-arse whose parents pushed her through so much Sunday selective-school tutoring that she got a scholar-ship, skipped a grade and was now, at age sixteen, in Year 12. 'No alcohol, except for ciders,' read the note. Donna O'Brian frowned at me from behind her freshly blow-dried golden hair and amber Gucci reading glasses. 'Does your mum know what ciders are?'

'Yes.' I tapped my bare foot impatiently on the marble floor. 'She only lets me drink ciders because they're low in alcohol.' This was obviously untrue. I had managed to convince my mum, prior to the party, that ciders were fizzy apple juice, no alcohol. Mum had dropped me at Pat O'Brian's triple-storey house with the note and clear no-alcohol instructions, before proceeding back to her 2002 Honda, parked across the road. She and Dad would sit there in the car, watching Viet-dramas until the end of the evening, the greenish glow of their iPad on their faces as they sucked on lychees, waiting to drive me home.

'Is your mum still here?' Donna frowned. 'Let me go find her.' In teeth-white sneakers, she chased Mum down the street, following Mum's floral-scented chestnut hair, navy blazer, Dior kitten heels.

I was not the only one trying to keep up.

Now I stood outside by the tennis courts, holding a Coke Zero. 'How did she not know ciders had alcohol?' Liam laughed.

'Does your mum even speak English?' Josh asked. He had a nose so big, he looked like a green-eyed hawk.

'No, she doesn't know anything. She thinks dead people can eat.'

'What?' Liam chuckled.

'Every week, she makes us go to the cemetery, so she can lay out food with chopsticks and we have to wait until my grandparents finish eating.' I did bunny ears around 'eating'.

'That's fucked.'

'Yes, she's so stupid.' I rolled my eyes. But as the words left my mouth, I felt the guilt of a raw egg crack inside my chest. The yolk was spilling out now, sickening me.

I had no idea who I had become.

————

Growing up, I hated the Vietnamese way of showing love. Mum would feed me banh xeo, chicken pho and lemongrass beef with turmeric rice, only to then stuff me with dessert – a variety of local Footscray market fruits, guava, durian and jackfruit. She never asked me anything more than two questions, 'Are you hungry?' and 'How are your grades?' All those dishes cost her a massive part of her meagre earnings as a St Albans travel agent. It also expended her time as a woman. As a mother, both time and money were commodities that she was ready to give up for me. Sacrifice and acts of service are the Vietnamese love languages.

However, going to a Catholic girls' school in Toorak, I was constantly surrounded by the privileged western way. I watched my friends run across the oval, wispy golden hair streaming across their freckled faces, muscular arms catching footballs or whipping tennis racquets with ease. Their parents allowed them to use their education for a holistically well-rounded life; they played sports, participated in debating competitions, argued with their parents over politics. My parents, in their naivety, only allowed me to use my education superficially, for an essay stamped with a big red 'A'. At dinner, in front of a Viet-drama, we ate our three-course meals silently. There was never any intellectual debate. As long as I got an A, my parents did not care about my thoughts on *To Kill a Mockingbird*, white heroism and the coexistence of good and evil, or *Of Mice and Men* and the correlation of companionship with the dangers of believing in the American Dream. To ask the right questions, I learned, is education, which is a privilege. My parents' minds were an $x + z + y^2 = a$. Sports, parties and friendships were all out of the equation. In my parents' algebra, there was school, there was family and there was the cemetery.

I ate my bun bo hue with one hand weakly holding red chopsticks and the other scrolling intently through Facebook. 'It's those white girls influencing you!' Mum yelled at me. 'I told you not to be friends with them, they are not like us!' She had found my C+ chemistry test hidden under Too Faced chocolate eye-shadow palettes and Tarte bronzers. Dad picked up my Young Adult novels, E. Lockhart's *We Were Liars*, Angie Thomas's *The Hate U Give*, and Ned Vizzini's *It's Kind of a Funny Story*, and ripped them, letters fluttering in the fish-sauce sky. 'It's these books, they feeding you bad ideas! All hates and lies and crazy.' Dad motioned a finger spinning cyclically beside his temples. 'Didn't I tell you not to read this? Didn't I tell you what to do? Just concentrate and get into medicine! Why do you keep having to bother us?' I ran upstairs sobbing, leaving my barely touched bun bo hue on the dining table, curly, caramel hair flopping behind me from an evening slept in braids.

At midnight, Mum opened my bedroom door. Outside, the moon was full as a mangosteen. My books were still scattered downstairs, facedown on the tiles, weeping with me. In the morning, they would be in our recycling bin, spines bruised. I pretended to sleep. But Mum knew better. She nudged me. In the dark, I slowly opened my eyes to a bowl of fresh dragon fruit. With a toothpick, Mum stabbed the fattest piece, pink flesh spotted with black freckles, and pushed it up to my face. The dragon fruit cost her $15 a kilo from the Footscray fruit markets – I saw it last Sunday, on our weekly cemetery fruit shop.

'Eat. We have to get into medicine.' My face was still red. I turned my head away, but Mum continued pushing the fruit to my mouth, incessant. I was not going to win this battle of the dragon fruit. I opened my mouth and let her push the segment between my teeth. I bit down slowly. My mouth filled with sweet juice.

———

At the cemetery, Mum looks at me from where she squats on the grave. 'Been a long time since you've come to see Ong Ba, huh? You miss us?' Young me would have said, I'm not visiting Ong Ba, they're dead, but older me is quiet, appreciating. The wind bloats my floral cotton blouse. I step away from the flowers, thumb rubbing the cool surface of my blue stone rings. It's been four years since I have been home.

In Sydney, where I have been living and studying, I have a lot of freedom. I have friends from law school who tell me 'that sucks' when I catch a cold or cannot sleep from anxiety, fuzzy eyes blinking at 4 am in a cold studio room. But it is my family who sends up jasmine tea for me, my mum who Uber Eats me pho. It is my family who, after all this time, welcomes me home …

In the cemetery, we are guided home to our ancestors, not with words, but with smells: the smoke of incense ash, the floral of jasmine tea, the coconut syrup of sticky rice on the tombstone. Incense ash falls on the granite tombstone. I wipe it off with a damp cloth. Dad stands behind me, face stern and unsmiling. But his eyes are soft. The corners of his pinkish lips curl up. His skin is creasing now, like sand dunes. When the sun shifts, it catches the blade of silver on his scalp. I pick up a mandarin and wipe it on my shirt. 'Are you hungry?' I give it to him.

Dad looks a lot skinnier now, like his body knows its time is coming, so it shrinks, prepares to make space for the next person. 'No, put it back,' he hisses. 'The incense hasn't fully burnt yet. Ong Ngoai is still eating.'

Mum picks up a spare mandarin from the basket. She wipes it on her coat. 'You hungry? You want this one?' I smile, eyes glassy. I haven't heard these words in a long time. 'No,' I say. 'I'm not hungry.'

The incense burns down to its red stick. Mum holds up the plate of soi, preparing to feed me like I am still a teen. Now that I am an adult, I can appreciate how our love is no longer one-dimensional, it expands, taking up the space of the abandoned cemetery. The cling wrap over the soi on my Ong Ngoai's grave, the smooth pearl of my mother's forehead, the crease of my father's dry hands … I grab the plate and chopsticks from my mother's aging palms. 'You eat,' I say, lifting a piece of soi to my mother's lips. When she bites down, her lipstick-stained mouth is speckled with grains.

I have a lot to learn from my mother.

Unplugged

Hannah McPierzie

It was my hands that gave me away.

I'd been doing so well up until that point. Relaxed face. Smiling. Probing questions. Nods of the head. Everything in order.

.

.

.

The operation was explained. The same process as last time; allow for fifteen hours in theatre, fat graft from my stomach to plug the wound, ICU.

Lots of big important words were used to disguise the plain reality – *this surgery will leave you completely deaf.*

.

.

.

.

.

.

.

.

.

But my hands.

The pen felt heavier than a sword.

Sweat pooled in my palms as a tremor started to find its rhythm.

'Just print your name, and date and sign here.'

So simple. How many times had I done that before? Almost daily. But not like this. Never like this.

.

.

.

My hands knew what they were being tasked with. That they were signing away my ability to hear. That they were consenting to make my ears obsolete; no more than hooks for my glasses to rest on.

.

.

.

.

.

.

.

.

.

.

.

.

Emergence

My eyes watched the ink trail out of the cheap, shitty biro. My ear heard the scratching and my throat constricted.

I couldn't help but think that a form like this deserved a fountain pen or a quill. Something with flourish and importance for what these words meant.

- .
- .
- .
- .
- .
- .
- .
- .
- .
- .
- .
- .
- .
- .
- .

I was embarking on a journey with one dimension removed. My emergence began with an emergency.

I started working on a list of all my favourite places. My plan was to visit and describe the sounds and noises for my future self to remember.

So I could sit in these places and 'hear' them.

So I wouldn't forget.

.

.

.

The docks down in Freo: seagull shrieks, tugboat horns, the clashing of sea containers being unloaded, waves breaking against hulls, water sloshing underneath.

.

A sound-photo of a familiar place.

.

.

.

It's strange.

.

.

.

.

.

.

Emergence

You'd think it would be all the beautiful sounds you'd miss, but I thought it would likely be the boring, mundane ones – traffic, building works, sirens, someone yelling, shopping centre music. They're the sounds that keep you connected to the world. Without them, what?

.

.

.

.

You're where?

.

.

.

.

.

.

.

.

.

.

.

.

.

.

Before surgery, I kept trying to envisage being deaf. I thought if I could get a handle on the logistics, I could make a plan and smooth the transition. Soften the fall.

.

.

.

But sticking your fingers in your ears or wearing noise-cancelling headphones doesn't come close to deafness.

.

.

.

There's no way of understanding that depth of silence. It's incomprehensible to a hearing person, because the world is constantly alive with sound.

.

.

.

.

.

.

.

.

.

.

.

Emergence

I am learning silence is different to quietness.

.

.

.

When something or somewhere is quiet, it usually means there's an absence or a reduction.

'The city was quiet today.'

It means that it's not normal. It's different to what you were expecting.

.

.

.

.

Silence though, that's a presence.

.

.

.

.

.

.

.

.

.

.

.

.

.

Silence is thick. It fills up the space in between things. It's otherworldly.

I can take my silence and throw it over me like a protective cloak. Sometimes I nest in there.

Tucked away. Unreachable.

Silence can be protective. It protects me.

-
-
-
-
-
-
-
-
-
-
-
-
-
-
-
-

Emergence

At other times, it prevents me.

.

.

.

The cloak turns to glass, and I am stuck on the other side of society.
Watching a world, soundless, within my jar.

A world I know is loud and diverse.

A world I never thought I'd live without.

.

.

.

I've begun to call these 'forcefield days' and 'jar days'.

.

.

.

.

.

.

.

.

.

.

.

.

At the beginning, it was mainly 'jar days'.

Months and months spent feeling like I was sitting inside my glass prison. Surrounded by uninterrupted, infinite silence. A spectator of life.

As time passes, I'm learning to reframe my perspective and see the silence as a forcefield. An invisible and impenetrable barrier: my own superpower emerging.

.

.

.

It takes time to find that strength within myself. I make progress while I sleep and my subconscious takes over, releasing thoughts and scenarios I try to hide from.

.

.

.

My darkroom days come back to me as I remember that you can't develop without processing.

.

.

.

.

.

.

.

.

Emergence

Immediately *after* surgery, my dreams were full of sound. Voices, laughter, music, bird song. The complete works. Normal. Up to that point in time.

.

.

Then, I would wake up.

The fuzzy transition into consciousness would end abruptly as the realisation took hold.

I was deaf.

.

.

.

Cold panic gripped me.
My breath quickened, as it tried to keep pace with my racing heart.
The floodgates opened and in poured anxiety.

.

.

.

.

.

.

.

.

.

.

All the questions and fears would hit me at once.

'What if the house catches fire?'

'How do I ask for help?'

'Will I ever make a new friend?'

'How do I *be* deaf?'

·

·

·

I tried my belly breathing. I tapped at my pressure points.
I journalled: dark, ugly words spewing out of me and onto a page.

·

·

·

When that didn't help, I took Valium.

·

·

Anything for some peace, a break from my own mind.
Sleep was to be avoided.

·

·

·

·

·

·

·

Emergence

After a while, I became deaf in my dreams, but I was still able to hear; in a way that only makes sense in a dreamscape. My mind processing a new identity, with a different reality.

.

.

.

I explained to people that I was now deaf, though I would be able to hear their voices.

.

.

.

I travelled to different parts of the world.

.

.

.

.

.

.

.

.

.

.

.

.

But.

.

.

.

.

I couldn't outrun the deafness.

.

.

.

It was my shadow.

.

.

.

.

.

.

.

.

.

.

.

.

.

.

Emergence

Gradually I lost sounds in my dreams. Traffic, birds, bustling streets. They all fell silent. Voices stayed for a long time.

.

.

.

I would often dream that there was a mystery frequency that I could miraculously hear. Music lived at this frequency, and I would get very excited hearing a favourite song. It would blast out of speakers and fill the air.

Suddenly I'd be surrounded by Bruce Springsteen or Jim Morrison and I wouldn't feel alone.

.

.

.

.

.

.

.

.

.

.

.

.

.

.

It was a lifeline. This safe, familiar cocoon that acknowledged I was deaf but still gave me sound.

.

.

.

Waking from these dreams was especially painful.

The half-awake fuzziness was fleeting as I remembered I was deaf and there was no frequency in this world that I could hear.

That felt cruel. Hard. Uncompromising.

.

.

.

.

.

.

.

.

.

.

.

.

.

Emergence

Nowadays I sign in my dreams.

.

.

.

Everyone in my dream does.

The man at Coles, the barista at the cafe, my doctors. Conversations in Auslan. Voices seen, not heard.

I'm not a minority in my dreams. We're all the same, though we're not all deaf.

.

.

.

I feel safe here.

.

.

.

Music comes and goes. Sometimes there, not always. I know that will disappear one day.

Maybe not entirely, but songs I loved will be forgotten and instruments muddled. It's a harsh reality, but it's mine to process.

.

.

.

.

.

Auslan stays with me as I wake to the silence and chat away to my husband. There's no draining panic or crash landing, just a fragile acceptance that my world is silent. I continue to try to reconcile the lack of sound with the knowledge that I still have a voice.

.

.

.

That silence doesn't mean silenced.

.

.

.

My first language has shifted from sound to sight.

.

.

Reading people's lips as they form their words. An accent detected through an unusual formation.

.

.

Emotion captured in the face sometimes betrays the words used.

.

.

.

.

Emergence

I like the tangibility of Auslan. It's active. You can't mindlessly bumble while scrolling through your phone. You have to be present, reading faces and watching words being carefully formed on hands.

.

.

.

My name is not a sound, but a shape, and I need to learn to recognise its form. The alphabet is spread over my fingers. My palms hold the subtleties of context and meaning. I take great comfort in the beautiful irony that my hands are no longer the killer of sound but the bringer of words.

Mayir

Geetha Pathanjali

'Are you sure?' my amma says in Tamil, razor in hand, plastic and pink.

'Just do it,' I say. I am twelve years old – right leg extended over the lip of the bathtub – and impatient. I am not practised at winning new freedoms and know that any one of them, once granted, can just as easily be taken away.

There is a slight friction as the razor glides over my soap-clad skin. Matted black hair peels off in thick wet clumps and falls to the bottom of the tub. It is my first taste of exercising agency over my body, and I like it.

'It's your mayir,' my amma had said an hour earlier. I was in my underwear, holding my tiny costume for the school play against my torso and eyeing the length of exposed limbs protruding from beneath it. 'You can accept it,' she had said, 'or you can do something about it.'

In sports class a few months later, I am sitting offside with Olivia Fulham, our legs outstretched in front of us in the school gym. She asks me if I wax or shave, and I shrug at her unconvincingly.

'I shaved, like, one time, I guess,' I say, like a cool girl, like I am in control of those dense, dark spores that slather my legs. Like I haven't spent every waking moment since that evening with my mother in the bathroom hatefully watching those piercing spikes breach the outer layers of my skin, day after day, no matter the pulling the plucking the pleading I give them.

I sneak a look at Olivia's legs, at the delicate golden-blonde down above her knees, near-invisible. She doesn't notice me looking; she has already turned back to the game.

In bed that evening, I lie awake and pretend I am someone else. A girl who is good, pretty and desirable. Skinny and hairless, without trying. It is many years before I realise that in my childhood fantasies I was never brown but white.

───────

I am twenty-three, waiting patiently on a fake-leather bed, naked from the waist down but for a loose white towel. A woman walks into the small cubicle. She chats to me like we are good friends as she readies her equipment. I resent her for the chatter, just as I would have resented an awkward silence. I smile back at her dutifully.

The wax is warm as she smooths it over the thick black hairs of my shin with a wooden spatula. She lays a strip of white cloth over the sticky clear-green layer, waits a moment and then rips it off in one expert motion, cloth, wax, hair and all. I try not to flinch from the pain, but I do, every time.

She frowns now, peering at my leg, and the questions begin.

'Have you shaved recently?' She applies more wax and rips another strip from my skin.

'No.' It's a lie. I have.

'And do you exfoliate?' Another strip; another hundred hairs rent from their follicles.

'Yes.' I think of the soppy, scratchy glove hanging untouched in the mould-ridden shower of my share house.

'Okay, well, you really need to moisturise.' Another one. It has a sound like the tear of fabric.

I nod, teeth gritted.

I walk out of the salon fifty minutes later, having paid one hundred and thirty-four dollars for the privilege of having every hair removed by the roots from my legs, my arms, my labia.

I don't know how to reconcile being a Strong Independent Woman with submitting my body to such an oppressive act, time and time and time again. The feel of my smooth legs afterwards is a drug. I am granted almost two full weeks before the familiar black spindles begin to show. I wear short skirts and feel the wind on my legs.

———

I meet Jack, and fall in love.

In quiet moments, he strokes the hair on my thigh into whorls with his finger. The trace of his touch on unruly strands leaves a gentle tingle.

I watch him and then sigh. 'I'm hairier than you even.'

'I love your hair,' he says. It's a matter-of-fact statement. His earnestness is unselfconscious; he is the kind of person that uses the word 'special' unironically.

Still, I don't believe him.

'But do you like it when I get a wax though?' I say.

'Yeah, I guess I like that too.'

'But do you like it better?' It's a trap. A lose–lose situation. We both know it.

He ponders the question.

'It's just … different.' He doesn't shrug, but it feels like he does, just the same.

That night, he tugs playfully at my pubes. It feels good. I giggle.

Over coffee, a friend suggests I try laser removal and I tell her I'll consider it. The idea of zapping my body hair into eternal oblivion – I have never wanted anything more – is tempting. But a part of me wonders if there might be a little less of me left afterwards, never to be found again.

When I get home I throw the laser removal flyer into the recycling bin.

———

Years pass and, over the lockdowns, my body hairs have a coming out. They explode riotously out of their follicles, one by one, unashamedly black on brown. They grow dense and long in every direction, and I let them be.

There is comfort in not seeing the known world, not facing its judgement, imagined or otherwise. On the first warm day of spring, I don my favourite skirt – a purple and yellow blossom-printed cotton midi.

Jack has lost his hat, and as we leave our apartment, he grabs one of mine from atop a shelf, navy blue and broad brimmed. I tell him I think it might be a woman's hat.

'I like it,' he says and puts it on his head. Confidence looks good on a person, I think to myself.

We walk, hand in hand, to a cafe a couple of blocks away.

The sun is on my face, and my hair – it rustles in the wind.

Renovations

Seth Malacari

'Don't you dare cut your fucking tits off.'

This threat came about four years ago, from my then-partner. A mutual friend had just had top surgery. I shook my head meekly, and squeaked out a 'No, never'. The instant I said it, I knew I was lying.

Prior to this, I'd never thought about transitioning. The furthest I'd stretched the boundaries of my gender was identifying as 'soft butch'. I cut my hair off at nineteen. A classic 'coming out as a lesbian' move. I have a slim frame and a small chest, and I played around with being 'androgynous', but I never imagined myself as male. I'd never let myself explore that desire.

There's this misconception that all trans people are born knowing they are in the wrong body. While this is the case for some folk, every person's journey is different. I came out at thirty-one. The process of realising I was trans was not a light bulb moment. It was more like individual fairy lights coming on one by one. Meeting people who identified as non-binary. Seeing trans guys on Instagram who were living their authentic selves. Putting socks in my jocks and realising I liked having a bulge. Going through a confusing time where I wasn't sure if I was attracted to men or wanted to be like them. One day I was at the beach straight after my shift at a cafe. The cafe was one of those places where you had to wear a collared shirt and pants, even in the middle of a Boorloo summer. I raced down to the beach and stripped off my clothes, and there was a moment that I stood bare chested, in between taking my uniform off and putting my swim top on. The sea breeze on my skin, the freedom of having nothing censoring me. The thrill of it. I still believe everyone should be allowed to go shirtless, but more than that, my breasts began to feel like another piece of unwanted clothing.

I was in an abusive relationship at the time these lights started coming on. I was stressed almost all of the time. Suicidal. I barely ate. I smoked. I was underweight, with almost no body fat on me at all. I wasn't a twig though. I was wiry. Muscular. When I saw photos of myself this way, I felt elated. Eating disorders are common in trans people. We try to control our bodies in any way we can. I didn't know this is what I was doing. All I saw was a body that didn't look female, as to me that made sense. I didn't understand myself any further than that at the time.

To realise I was trans, I needed a healthy environment where I felt safe and free to explore my gender identity, which only came after leaving that bad relationship, plus I needed role models. I needed representation. And that representation didn't come for me until I was well into adulthood.

Don't get me wrong, I had a great childhood. Middle-class suburbia. Excelled at sports, and at school. Parents still together. Pool in the backyard. A Tamagotchi that always died. What was missing was any sort of queer representation. There was this show in the nineties, *The Secret World of Alex Mack*, about this girl who had a chemical spilled on her and developed cool powers. She wore baggy skate clothes and a backwards cap. She was everything to me. Alex (which is arguably the number one choice of name for trans men in western society) is queer coded in so many ways, but there's no actual mention of being queer in the show. I saw this show and wanted to be a cool skater kid with a backwards cap and to change my name to Alex. I didn't think of those things as 'boy' things. I just saw something that appealed to me. If even one show I'd seen back then had featured a trans kid, and not in a 'dude in a dress as a punchline' kind of way, I might have clocked on to this a whole lot sooner. Even today, trans people in the media are still wildly under-represented. This is why I write. So that some kid can see themselves reflected in my stories and have the language to explore their gender identity. To know that it is OK, and they are not alone.

I sometimes wish I'd come out earlier. Mainly so I could have avoided the early 2000s trend of over-plucking my eyebrows. I still have a bald patch in one of them. Since starting testosterone, I have grown hair in every place on my body except this one patch of eyebrow. It would also have been nice to start my adult life with my actual name, and not my deadname. I legally changed my name months ago and so far I've updated three out of the thirty million places I need to update. I didn't go with Alex in the end. I chose to keep my first initial the same, so I didn't have to change my signature. Also, my sister's boyfriend's name is Alex, and I thought that might be a little weird.

On the other hand, if I'd transitioned sooner I wouldn't have my daughter.

She's six. She recently asked me, 'Dad, do you wish you'd been born a boy?'

I told her no, because then she wouldn't exist. To be clear: trans men can give birth. Trans men can have their eggs implanted into a womb-owning partner, or surrogate. But for this particular kid, had I transitioned, say, as a teen, my life would be much different and the exact egg to donor sperm combo that made her likely would not have happened. After some awkward explaining about the role of sperm, she happily accepted this reasoning and then asked to play Barbies. Which we did. Because I'm a cool dad.

When I was ready to come out, just one year ago, I told my girlfriend first. I was a bit of a coward about it. I texted her, heart racing, something like, 'Would you still love me if I was a boy?' My girlfriend, who was at work at the time, replied, 'Of course babe, I love you no matter what.' So, in my mind, I was thinking, OK, I've done it, I've come out, everything is great.

That night, I was at home scrolling Reddit for info on starting hormones, binding, packing, top surgery. The works. I was making a list of new names on my phone. I was staring at myself in the mirror and frowning. My girlfriend comes home, sees what I'm up to and, folks, here is when the importance of NOT sending vague text messages to announce significant news becomes clear. My previous experience in relationships had made me reluctant to discuss my gender, so this day was the first she was hearing about the possibility of me being transgender. Understandably, she had not realised that my text was more than an extrapolation of the 'Would you still love me if I was a worm?' thing other couples do. Safe to say, she was more than a little blindsided.

After some back and forth in which I essentially asked her to process in ten minutes what I had spent the last thirty-one years processing, all was well. Her initial response remains true, she does love me no matter what. I try to remember that even though transitioning is so deeply personal, it does still impact those around us. It's easy to get wrapped up in it, especially at the beginning when everything is new and exciting. That same beginning for partners, parents, or even friends, can be the total opposite. They are experiencing a transition of their own, one that they've had a whole lot less time to prepare for. In saying that, if the people in your life don't accept you, walk away. Trans people deserve to be loved as their whole self.

Transitioning is not a one-step process, nor is it the same for everyone. I compare it to doing a DIY renovation on a house you inherited. You have a house that's not quite right. Maybe you absolutely hate it, but the market is terrible right now, so you have to live in this house. You sit down and envision your dream house. You spend a lot of money, and it takes several years. Things will go wrong. Perhaps the paint colour isn't quite what you imagined. I had dreams of being a handsome man with a dark beard, but, as it turns out, I'm a handsome man with a ginger beard. And while all this renovation is going on, people are stopping by your unfinished house to ask questions and gawk at you. In the end, your home might not match the original plans, but it's something you're proud of, hopefully. I'm still working on my house. I'll let you know how it turns out.

I'm still emerging. But I'm happy. I'm me. I'm writing this today after getting a fresh haircut at the barber. I'm wearing a chest binder. I'm avoiding going to the licensing centre to update my driver's licence, because you have to do it in person, and I hate doing things in person. And I'm getting ready to go to meet with my plastic surgeon.

That's right: I'm going to cut my fucking tits off.

An ode to Shandy, wherever she may be

Nina Angstmann

There is a moment, between the inhale and the exhale, where time stops. A millisecond of weightlessness. I yearn for the bliss point. My appointment book is red, full for the day, and overloaded with walk-ins. I'm running thirty minutes behind already, partly due to a printer jam and partly due to the suicidal adolescent who entered under the guise of a pill script, a fortunate pick-up. Fix fix fix. All in fifteen minutes. Eyes closed, I move the stethoscope methodically around. Breathe in, and out. And in, and hold, and out. I repeat this more times than technically necessary. With every exhale I feel – something – more grounded? Reassured? That when all around you is crumbling, the certainty of the inhale and exhale continues?

Sometimes the bliss moment coincides with the pause between heartbeats – eyes half closed, I am far away. I notice a suspicious mole on my patient's back and am unceremoniously yanked back to the fluorescent lights of the consulting room. Shit. I think Mrs Brown has a melanoma. The next few patients are really going to give it to me now.

And he's going to be angry. I'll be home late.

———

Walking on eggshells is exhausting, but I do not yet know this is the name for my reality. My bones are tired, and I am living in a heavy, grey fog.

———

On the third attempt, I made it inside the police station. Or rather, I was dragged by a well-meaning colleague. I was in my lycra uniform – activewear, my modern-day armour. The junior constable looked barely old enough to have stubble. 'But you don't look like the sort of victim we usually see around here,' he said, glancing at my Mimco handbag. I walked out.

———

Her name is Shandy. Her hair is blue, she works at Centrelink, and she saved my life, though she does not know this. For her, it was probably another day on the Centrelink call desk.

Line up, take a number. I had been in line in the queue for close to an hour. I recognised three of my patients in the line ahead of me. They did not recognise their doctor. Pregnant. Again. Unable to work. Extricating from a living nightmare I didn't know I was in. The magnitude of what lay ahead, the hopelessness of it all. Trapped. The shame. Should I have stayed? Can I just press control Z? Undo? Couldn't I have just walked on eggshells better, longer, faster, harder? I can't do this. I can't carry on. I have failed the growing life inside me. My medical brain starts racing – road trauma, insulin overdose, opioids, antihypertensives. So many exits.

She calls my name. The tears spill over and I start sobbing. There is a fake plant next to her computer. She tells me financial information about crisis payments, single parent benefits and services I can access. I don't remember anything she says. Then she leans forward and takes my hand. She whispers to me, 'You can do this,' as she hands me tissues. 'I've been there too. You'll look back on this one day. You're doing this for your babies. Just do the next right thing.'

I found out months later that a Shandy is a beer, mixed with sweet lemonade.

———

Court is a blur. I swear to tell the truth, the whole truth and nothing but the truth. I'm holding my daughter's favourite Elsa card, from *Frozen*. Elsa knows how to let it go. Be like Elsa. Be Elsa. The cold doesn't bother her anyway. I also swear that as long as I live, I will never again be in the witness box in a courtroom.

An interim domestic violence order is granted.

———

When I am admitted to hospital with complications in the pregnancy, they ask me to pick my own pseudonym. It's the protocol for patients in my situation, the nurse tells me, for protection. In another life, I might have chosen something fabulous, like a gaudy stage name, or a French nom de plume. But right now, my mind is blank. I can't think of anything and don't know who I am anymore. I don't want to be on this protocol. They call me Jane Doe.

———

The judgement is delivered. I am able to lawfully relocate, far away. My lawyer tells me to leave immediately, before a stay order can be issued. With my toddler in the back seat, my unborn baby in my belly and my medical degree in the boot, I drive into the night. I take nothing else. I do not stop until I have crossed the border. My chariot is a thirteen-year-old dented Mazda. Only the stars know where I am now.

———

The first time I received a charity hamper of donated toys for the children, I cried with joy. We danced around and tossed them in the air. I half expected to see some of the things I myself had donated to St Vinny's over the last few years.

———

One year passes. Unemployed. Raising babies. Surviving. Breathing. Inhale. Exhale. Minute-by-minute compartments most days. Inhale. Exhale. Not thriving. Women's group, art therapy, domestic violence recovery group, social workers, high-risk post-natal group, Centrelink. Being me has become a full-time job. I need something that is not about me to feed my racing mind in the awake hours. Inhale. Exhale. Can I ever be a doctor again? The social worker says I have to learn to fix a bar in my shark tank, to learn to keep out sharks. How can I be qualified to fix other people when my own shark tank is a dud? Inhale. Exhale. My brain is Peppa Pig, op shops and free local council community events. I enrol in an online diploma in child health.

———

I finally bought a TV. I saved up for a few months. As I flicked the channels for the first time, I found SBS. Documentaries. Foreign language films. I cackled in glee. I am free to control the remote. A piece of me that had long been buried clicked back into place.

———

I give a speech at my best friend's wedding. About healthy love. Trees that grow tall, but neither in each other's shadow. Strong roots. Growing taller because they are together. For the first time, I actually believe what I am saying. I crumble when I read the part of the wedding invitation I wasn't meant to see – in lieu of gifts, please donate to domestic violence services for women and children. She never even told me.

———

My grandfather, a Polish World War II survivor, once told me, when he was alive – they can take away your house, they can take away your family, they can take away your job. They can take away every object you own. But nobody can ever, ever take away your education.

I hang my medical degree on the wall in my single bedroom rental and peruse online courses.

———

One. Two. Three fabulous women from my year in medical school have contacted me in the last month – word has clearly gotten out about my deviation from perfection, my fall from grace, and they too want advice about leaving their similar situations. I wonder if it's a coincidence they're all GPs too. Fixers. You'd never know it from the outside, perfectly made up and the usual lycra uniform. Ironically, the three were the brightest, most clever shining stars in medical school. Do you think they intentionally pluck the fanciest feathers for their hat? I help the first, and the second. By the third, I am done. I have paid it forward and I must stop now, it is time to live forward and not look back. It feels like I'm now part of some sort of Avon pyramid scheme for healthcare professionals who are navigating their exits from violence in their own homes. I pass on the contact details for the First to the Third. She will be OK.

———

I study secretly. I am awake. I am alive. My mind is alive. I am glad to be alive. The legalese of criminal law and forensics comes easily to me. The medicine all comes back to me. The ethical issues turn on a light in my brain. I can't stop reading – case law, forensic principles, ethical conundrums, privacy principles, injury interpretation, medical injustices. I have found my why.

———

I wonder if they know I'm wearing a Vinny's shirt in my job interview. My words feel unnatural – clunky and childlike. I've not had a professional conversation in years. Peppa Pig, nappies and nursery rhymes are all I know. I feel like an imposter. They ask me if I'll be tempted to rescue criminals and bring them home with me. Absolutely not, I respond with certainty. I am no longer a fixer. It is not my obligation to fix. I don't tell them I have children. I know how the world works now for single mothers.

———

Emergence

I work. I work hard. I work day and night. Every time my on-call phone rings – a sexual assault to attend, a physical violence case to photograph and document – I am grateful I have purpose. And I am good at what I do. In the middle of the night, through weary eyes and coffee shots, I drive from police station to police station, hospital to hospital. I am busier on warm nights, balmy nights. Cold and rainy nights seem to keep violence somewhat at bay. Or do people just not report on those nights? My Mazda again becomes my chariot. Together we drive until dawn, from sexual assault to sexual assault. Street violence, rape, domestic violence, bruises, strangulation, collecting DNA swabs, clothing, photographs, documenting the stories of the worst day in the life of strangers. But these are problems too great to fix. I am not a fixer. I am there to sit with that stranger in the darkness of their darkest day. It is my job to be an advocate for truth.

———

I have been out all night attending cases. Homicide, sexual assault. Collecting DNA samples from battered and weary bodies, so science can speak the truth. My mother is sleeping on the couch at home with the children. It is 7 am, she calls and asks if I will be home soon, as the children would like croissants from the bakery please, not the plain croissants but the ones with the chocolate in the middle.

———

I need a new car. My boot is completely full with the pram and nappies. I have the sexual assault kits wedged between the two car

138

baby seats. My eldest has started using the sexual assault kit as a stable table to do her colouring.

———

It is Christmas. I decorate the tree with the children. I start my own traditions. The children get one Christmas ornament each year, reflecting something they accomplished that year. My son got a book ornament, as he learned to read. Ballet slippers for my daughter. We sing carols, loudly, and drape distastefully excessive amounts of fairy lights over the tree. I hang my ornament – a magnificent blue glittery dove with wings spread, in flight.

I add a slosh of lemonade to my beer, and raise a toast to Shandy.

———

I am sitting outside the Supreme Court. I am giving expert evidence in a case. I am here to educate the court. I am here with detached objectivity. I am here to assist the court in determining truth.

———

There is a moment, between pushing the shutter button down and releasing it, where time stops. A millisecond of weightlessness. I take photos of the victims' faces first, for identification purposes. I am behind the camera. The victims hold up a colour chart under their chin, ironically like a mug shot. Click. Some look down, tears streaming over their black eyes and down their bruised cheeks. Some reflexively break into a smile, an uncontrolled, conditioned response to having a giant SLR camera pointed at their face. But most, once I am hidden behind the camera, for that brief millisecond, meet my gaze through the viewfinder.

Release. Click. Release. Their eyes are empty and deep and desperate and ashamed and terrified. Click. I hope they find their Shandy. Release.

Eleanora

Alex Chan

Mum and I return to Melbourne on a cloudy spring day pierced by a chilly wind that hints of the receding winter. I am seven years old, drowsy from the long flight and scared of this unfamiliar place that was 'home'. I feel like I should remember more of Melbourne, and my stomach lurches as I see the foreboding storm clouds gathering over the city as we land. All I can think about is that we have left my dad behind – and the only life I remember – far across the ocean in Malaysia.

The unit we move into is cavernous compared to the cramped, stacked highrise condominiums in Kuala Lumpur. I learn that it is considered small compared to the imposing bungalows that line the leafy streets of Mont Albert, but walking up and down the corridors, the unit feels empty and silent without the constant buzz of my dad's TV emanating from the living room, or without his footsteps echoing as he lumbers through the hallways.

In the first few months, I petition my mum for a dog. We have arrived midway through the school year, so I am passing the time until the next one by reading, playing ball games against myself and piling up huge phone bills sending mostly unanswered texts to my dad. These activities do not quell the pit of loneliness that has been growing in my stomach.

Emergence

Mum, stressed from the move into single parenting, and readjusting to life in Australia, negotiates with me and we compromise on a plant. Just to start off with, until we're both sure that I can bear the responsibility of looking after a dog. A trip to Bunnings yields seeds for a flowering purple and yellow plant. I am unspeakably excited as we plant the seeds in the small patch of dirt outside the unit, and for weeks I eagerly and dutifully check for signs of life twice a day. When I notice small green shoots poking through the soil, I can hardly contain myself – I am entranced by the colourful flowers that the plant yields, and Mum teaches me to handle the petals and leaves gently as they bloom. I decide to name it Eleanora and I check on her every day until I start school.

The summer I start school is sweltering and oppressive. We are in a drought and everything feels dry and dusty. I am not used to the burn of the sun and slink through the trees lining the primary school instead of climbing and running and playing with the other girls. Not, I come to realise, that many of the other girls want to play with me anyway. From the first day, I have stood out in the small class, with an accent I'd never noticed before, completely dwarfed in my school uniform, and sporting an unflattering bob haircut beloved by my mother and other Chinese mothers of her generation. Even aged eight, the viciousness of an all-girls school is palpable, and soon I am spending classes in silent tears and lunchtime shrinking away from the sun and the laughter of my classmates. I burn with shame when my dad calls and asks if I have made any new friends.

I am climbing the steps to the front door one day after school when I spot Eleanora wilting and slumped in the heat. Her flowers lie crumpled in the dirt around her, flashes of colour piercing through the dark, dry soil. Her leaves are curled inwards, protecting themselves from the glare of the rays relentlessly bearing down upon her. I am utterly distraught.

My mum finds me an hour later, curled up in bed sobbing hysterically, unable to deal with the crushing guilt of killing Eleanora. Mum tells me that this is a sign that I wasn't ready to take responsibility for a pet, but I am too upset to care: I don't want a dog anymore, I just want Eleanora to be OK. She is my only friend here in this forbidding and unfriendly country that is now my home.

Every night for the next month, I sneak outside after dark, feeling like a criminal under Melbourne's drought laws, in my hands a plastic bottle of water caught from my four-minute shower, and I feed Eleanora, who drinks with relief. One weekend I even construct a small tarp to shelter her from the sun. She thrives underneath this attention, and within a few months I am showing her off to Romy, a round-cheeked Australian girl from school who shared her Vegemite Saladas with me. Two friends now.

When we move out three years later, I take some time to say goodbye to the little plant that I nearly killed. Eleanora has grown now, budding bright flowers, reaching for the sky, leaves unfurled for the world to see. She's beautiful, and I leave with a smile.

———

'If you look after it really well, it might even grow some flowers!'

I am twenty-one and a potted succulent is being thrust in my face as a housewarming gift. I've been living in London for almost a year and, having just finished my master's degree, under the UK's restrictive immigration policies, am in danger of being forced out of the country I have called my new home for five years. I am confronted with the revelation that I can't get a sponsored job in the music industry and the fact that I will eventually have to face down the family members who told me a music degree was worthless when I first set out to do it. I have decided to interrupt the tedium and melancholia of job rejections with a party. My flatmate is thrilled by the gift and promises to take care of it. I haven't owned a plant since Eleanora.

The party is a blur of familiar faces. I can't tell if the warmth I am feeling is Asian alcohol flush or genuine affection for the people laughing and dancing with me. Every day I am haunted by the possibility of leaving them and I already grieve the loss, dreading the distance of these friends who have carried me through the last five years. My visa expiration has loomed like a shadow over the last year, weighing me down even as I celebrate and revel in my life in London. I so desperately yearn for this country to want me as much as I want to stay.

The succulent sits in the sole sun-dabbled corner of our basement flat, a small nook next to the backdoor, just in my line of vision as I sit at the dining table, desperately searching for a job that will allow me to continue my life here. This is where I feel I can see the next five years stretching ahead like a road for the first time. I religiously water the succulent, watch the water soak into the soil, the excess spilling over the edge of the pot like a waterfall.

It finally dies at the end of summer, a long and drawn-out process that feels like a betrayal. I have now started applying for jobs outside the music industry, something I had sworn could never possibly happen, and the plant dying feels like an omen.

My flatmate and I desperately try to resurrect the succulent with plant food, a bottle of very expensive 'rejuvenating water' we found in the closest garden centre and frantic Google searches about succulent wellbeing. In spite of our best efforts, the succulent sounds its death knell, unable to survive the damp, moist British climes, so different from the dry and balmy deserts of Mexico. Or so we thought.

One more Google diagnosis: cause of death was over-watering. Turns out succulents can thrive in the UK, if they are lucky enough.

'We loved it too much!' my flatmate wails. 'We tried too hard!'

By contrast, I can barely muster a shred of sympathy for it before I throw it in the garden waste. I tell myself that I wouldn't have been able to take it home with me through Australian customs anyway, when I get kicked out of the UK.

———

I watch fondly as my partner breaks the earth of our garden for the first time. I am twenty-seven and observing him from inside our new unit in Melbourne as I lean against the kitchen counter, basking in a ray of sunlight. I feel the stress of my time in London and the frenzy of our mid-pandemic move across the world melting away.

'We'll grow a herb garden!' he had declared months earlier, poring over the pixelated floor plans of our first home together. 'Thyme, rosemary, mint, oregano, basil ...'

'Is mint a herb?' I wondered.

He had waxed lyrical about his vision for a vegetable patch, how he would put seeds down before winter arrived, how next summer he could see us sipping fresh mint tea on the patio with leaves he would cultivate, how in ten years' time I could bake tart with the lemons from the young tree we had just bought. These dreams of the future were tangible in a way that they could never have been if we had stayed in our damp basement flat in London, miserably trying to maintain a pathetic herb garden in the small slab of concrete we called our backyard.

Doubts about uprooting our modest life in London had still crossed my mind even as we landed in Melbourne that previous autumn and found ourselves weaving through the tree-lined streets of the eastern suburbs. The pangs of familiarity I felt as we drove past the rusted iron gates of my high school clashed with the shock of seeing the gleaming new skyscrapers of Box Hill that had risen during my eight years away. They now towered over the aging shopping centre I remembered. The old music shop where I had taken my first violin lesson was replaced by a real estate agent advertising sparkling apartment blocks in its windows. Our old block of units, the one Mum and I had moved into when we had returned to Melbourne, had been demolished and replaced with a beige mansion fronted with Roman-style columns. I wondered what had happened to Gwenda, the caring British woman who lived in the front unit, and whose son Stuart had helped me pick out Eleanora at Bunnings.

But, I realised, as I stepped out of the car outside Mum's new house, the crisp Melbourne air was still sweet and fresh, the magpies still gathered on the nature strip, and the autumn leaves still floated to the ground and coloured the streets with a warm auburn hue. In the early morning sun, I pieced together the fragments of the Melbourne I remembered.

I had looked at my partner, expecting to see apprehension or trepidation. I may have been returning home, but he was abandoning the only life and country he had ever known, just as I had done once, long ago. But – he smiled, squeezed my hand and stepped forward towards our new lives without hesitation.

More than a year ago now. Here we are, putting down roots in a place I have always called home, that once felt so foreign but now feels both old and new and exciting. For the first time, I feel neither the haunting of my past childhood in Kuala Lumpur nor the allure of adventure and precarity in London. Melbourne is where I have landed with both feet on the ground and eyes on the horizon. For the first time, calling it 'home' is right.

As spring begins, I can see small sprigs of mint emerging from the soil. My partner is elated and pulls me into a dance around our table. As he goes out to harvest the spoils of his hard work, the first yield of many, the future stretches out in front of me like the sky.

Come out swinging

Miranda Jakich

Dear sis

My day, your night – we bat between time zones in a game of long-distance ping-pong. I'm still waiting for the day you figure out that 4 am is not a good time for me.

What I can't see, I can imagine. Come morning, you'll brush fairy dust from your eyes, hurl the alarm across the room and stumble to the bathroom, your styled American hair intact. How I envy your legendary knack for deep, easy slumber – in fetal curl at a busy airport, a couch in a nightclub, a power nap at the side of the motorway. Sleep has never been my friend. Lately, I plump my pillow and watch the pendulum swing for hours. My brain is an electrical fuse box, firing a thousand amps into the night.

There's something on my mind that I need to share with you. 'When will you tell her?' I get asked. The lily-livered voice in my head whimpers, 'Maybe never.' Fellow travellers as tight as we are shouldn't have secrets, but each time I try to tell you, the words stick on my tongue. If courage makes a queen out of a slave, I'm doomed to servitude.

My nigra is in trouble. It may sound like an exotic travel destination like Costa del Nigra or a trendy name for dark chocolate.

In fact, the substantia nigra lives in all of us, taking pride of place in the central brain, home to dopamine cells, important for sending signals to our body like 'climb those stairs' or 'pluck that coin from your wallet'. Over time, predatory T-cells have been hitting on my unarmed dopamine. My besieged nigra has shed cells like a withered rose drops its petals. A rich brown nerve centre that once transmitted infinite signals to the body is now a stranded vacant grey mass – a 'nigra nulla'.

Early signs that something was wrong were struggling to zip up Mum's jacket, and the sensation that my feet were glued to the ground. Easily brushed off with perfectly logical explanations – that deadpan stare admired by work colleagues because it freaked management in meetings: a tactic nobody else could mimic; the stooped walk: a family trait, as Grandfather swept the pavement with his chin; the croaky voice, once described as a dying tadpole – well, what do you expect from the daughter of a toneless man who butchered 'You are my sunshine'? The wobbly balance: a twin to hearing loss; the tremors and anxiety: stress from bone-deep trauma.

A petri dish of symptoms and theories – but all dead wrong. Until the day a neurologist named it and stuck it to my brow. 'You have Parkinson's, a progressive neurodegenerative disease.' Slap. 'When you came in the door, I noticed your mask-like face and rigid posture, and you weren't swinging your arms.' Slap again. Without biomarkers, lab tests or brain scans, that's how diagnosis unfolds for this illness, leaving you holding a wildcard, as no two people have the same risk, onset or progression. Straight into denial – 'It must be stress.' Nope. Different red flags.

'Stress doesn't produce symptoms like small handwriting, slow movement, or freezing when you climb out of a car.'

He said that age and Parkinson's don't go well together, as if red wine doesn't pair well with oysters. And then the biggest slap of all … 'You've probably got ten years left in the mainstream.'

'I don't like the sound of that,' the tremor in my voice far worse than the tremor in my pinkie. 'What does that actually mean?'

'Exactly that. You have ten years left in the mainstream.'

The opaque soothsayer left my imagination to join the dots. I felt like a child who'd had the candy snatched from her hand.

I channelled Dad – our very own king of denial, convinced he was invincible. He would have snorted, 'What's old age got to do with it? And what's this mainstream? Where people swim?' Dad, as you know, lived his life dominating the mainstream, with his booming voice and boundless self-belief, sucking the oxygen out of every space he occupied.

Remember that time I told him even he couldn't live forever, and he fired back, 'Bah! Watch me try.' Well, I'm not like Dad, lording his way through life in robust health, and it's hard to feel cocky when your brain cells are vanishing.

Who to blame? Science is still guessing but points to nerve toxins like air pollution, pesticides and chemicals, as well as stress and genetics. I suspect Mum, the hygiene queen, with her penchant for industrial-strength cleaning agents. What about all that hairspray? Round and round her head until her hair became a solid helmet. It burned my nostrils in the next room; I hate to think what it did to hers. Dad doesn't escape suspicion either. He was liberal with Roundup weed killer and Yates dust, snuffing out the aphids on his tomatoes, then, in his final dementia years, spraying WD-40 on the BBQ 'to give the sausages a nice kick'.

Maybe it's the flatmate who doused the floor with Baygon to stop cockroaches crawling into our beds. Or unavoidable microplastics – might as well undress and roll around in landfill.

Maybe, maybe ...

Our urban and rustic lives are littered with malignant culprits. I read that farmers in regional vineyards have the highest rates of Parkinson's in France, ingesting poison so we can drink wine. Toxins are so rife, it's surprising we haven't all got two heads and green skin.

Then there's genetic mutation. I may carry the genetic baton passed to me by Grandfather and Uncle, all the way from Croatia.

My neurologist says genes only account for fifteen per cent of cases, and treatment is the same regardless of cause, 'so don't overthink it'. But all mention of genetic research on Google is a magnet for my eyeballs.

Medication helps manage my symptoms. Once Parkinson's overwhelms this course, I'll upscale to a drug called Levodopa. In time, each drug is just more weak tea; that's why we need a cure. You always encouraged me to move more; well, I'm boning up on exercises that rewire the brain. Meds and movement is the mantra. 'No supplements unless you want to empty your wallet' – a rum statement from a textbook practitioner at rehab, looking straight at me, dismissing cannabis oil, turmeric, and – let's get crazy – maqui berry and mucuna. So tempting to tell him I practise mysticism and animal sacrifice by moonlight, quaffing down fresh blood to replenish my inner nigra.

Emergence

Rehab is where I met my new tribe. Their voices, soft and flat, collapse like fallen souffles. I shout to show this disease who's boss. Our physiotherapist pumps us to 'move big', 'speak loud' and, of course, 'swing those arms'. We're encouraged to be powerful 'warriors', fighting back instead of resigning ourselves to an inevitable trajectory. This disease has a master plan to turn us into small, stooped ghosts, unconfident, hiding at home and giving up. For 200 years, there was no pushback, but the worm has turned. As the baby in the group, I get a preview of what could lie ahead, as well as inspiration for 'living brave'. Take Albert, in his nineties, smashing it on the exercise bike, solving word puzzles as he spins. Angie in ballet tights, determined to win a tango trophy before her eightieth birthday. Bewitching Margot, backing her walker over my toes as she hurries home to her third boyfriend in two years, pushing past Brigitta, author of a new book. I'd say that's all pretty impressively mainstream, wouldn't you?

We share our experiences with orthodox medicine and follow the research, sifting out the quackery and snake oils, to find those few nuggets of gold. A new language binds us.

Neuroplasticity, dyskinesia (involuntary movements), bradykinesia (slowness, freezing), idiopathic (cause unknown), dysphagia (difficulty swallowing), dysarthria (speech and voice problems), apraxia (closing eyelids) – all bread and butter words in this new world of mine. They roll off my tongue as easily as 'Pass the salt please'.

I won't kid you – living with Parkinson's is no side hustle. There are forty possible symptoms, and I'm familiar with twenty. They can be pesky, like restless legs; quirky, like acting out my dreams; even absurd, like getting tangled up in jacket sleeves; or spoilers, like migraines, insomnia and fatigue. New ones spring up overnight, like my splutter cough and breathlessness as Parkinson's stiffens the muscles in my airways and chest wall. It's a sneaky disease, creeping up from behind with a few subtle symptoms, then bolder and more aggressive: scornful and mocking as it peels strips off your identity. I dread cog fog, hallucinations and losing my sense of taste so I can't tell an orange from a fishcake. Please, not those.

The thief has already taken my voice, my smile, so the mirror reflects an avatar in a video game. I may sound normal on WhatsApp thanks to voice therapy, but I keep my conversations short at the first sign of a croak. I miss my old self, the textured voice, animated face, brisk gait. I long to smell flowers, my own cooking, even my whiffy garbage. What will it steal from me next?

Parkinson's prepped me for a global pandemic that forced us all to make changes to our lives. I already knew what it was like to be up-ended by something I never saw coming. My radius shrank before lockdowns turned all our homes into holding pens where we squinched down, leg-cuffed in a blue funk. Sorrow for my afflicted nigra melded with global grief, loneliness and anxiety. Suddenly my greatest heartache was not Parkinson's and mourning for what my future could have been; it was being kept apart from you.

I still have all the same plans, like laying our parents' ashes to rest in Croatia, you by my side; breaking bread with family and friends in New Zealand; your delayed wedding in New York.

My neuro has given me the green light to travel in our pandemic world because my risk factor is 'only fractionally higher' than a healthy person's. So, you see, Parkinson's and a pandemic have not scuppered our plans, just put a wrinkle in them.

The off-the-grid vibe really suits me now – no deadlines, dressing to impress, rushing and multi-tasking like a spinning top. My neurologist's 'bye-bye mainstream' prediction doesn't scare me anymore. I've emerged past his clinical prognosis into a new kind of mainstream that glimmers with hope and promise. Anyway, he's not God, and, in a decade, I may do a victory lap in his clinic, arms swinging, dressed like Madonna.

Now that I've told you the truth about my substantia nigra, I might out her to the world, in the gentlest possible way. She should not be a shameful secret, kept in darkness and fear. Her passing is more than a lament about a villain and its victim. She is the surprising key that has unlocked new wisdom and a different way of being.

Parkinson's may bookend this last chapter of my life but it will not have the last word and skittle me. I intend to live well, have purpose and reclaim some power. It is billed as the 'stubborn enemy of science', yet science will boot this disease right off the planet. It just takes one tweak of a molecule or peptide – and there springs hope for a future breakthrough.

When I see you, there will be no icky surprises. I'll do my absolute best to flex my frozen face and break out the old smile at your wedding. Parkinson's may lay claim to every part of me – my limbs, my lungs, my brain – but it cannot touch my heart, and that is where you are.

When you're ready, bat that ping-pong ball right back, and bat it hard and strong. I'll be waiting to hear your voice – even if it's four in the morning.

Sydney, 2022

Truffled feathers

Chenturan Aran

The special was duck fried rice with truffle oil.

$20?

I thought truffles were the Rolls Royce of fungi? I heard they were like mushrooms, but instead of caps they had top hats and were covered in jewels rather than spots.

'I don't eat duck,' Amma chimes.

I checked to see if truffle was spelt with one 'f', kinda like 'Rebok' shoes at a Bali street stall. Nope. Two 'f's. Twenty dollars made no sense.

'Chicken fried rice,' Amma says. I push a basket of prawn crackers in front of her.

The chef must be dropping the truffle oil with a pipette. A single drop can go a long way. A drop of LSD can give you an out-of-body experience. It can make you writhe on the floor and speak in tongues. I bet a drop of truffle oil will straighten your posture and have you saying affluent words like 'trite' and 'gravitas'. Hell, maybe it's a psychedelic truffle. Maybe once I have a spoonful of this psilocybin fried rice, space–time will melt. Maybe the tablecloth will drip fabric and turn the entire carpet into a lake of white cotton that'll slither up the walls and chairs, and over the prawn crackers, and up the legs of the lovers at table 13, who will turn into tablecloth sculptures suffocating on each other's cotton tongues. Maybe I will see that all matter is connected by a single underlying fabric. I will transcend separateness, and yet, with the truffle, I will also transcend income brackets, and the white cotton skin of everything will turn brown, and then leather, and the repeating gold pattern of the Louis Vuitton logo will wallpaper itself over reality until I'm ensconced in a designer suitcase. That's all I want from this meal. To feel like the world is a designer suitcase being dragged by a divine Kardashian gliding through a cosmic terminal. Is that too much to ask?

'No duck,' says Amma.

'Why?'

'I don't eat duck.'

'Since when?'

'Chicken.'

'No.'

'Duck vendaam.'

'Why?'

'Chicken.'

'The duck and the chicken are cousins. That's like saying you'd eat Karunyan but not Vathsan.'

'I don't eat duck.'

'I want it.'

'I don't eat duck.'

'I want it!'

Now, I could order the truffle fried rice and substitute chicken for duck, but rearranging a delicacy isn't classy. That's not the truffle mentality. See, Amma doesn't understand high society, which is why she's eating her sixth prawn cracker.

'Amma, I want the duck.'

'Chenturan.'

'You're crazy. I want it.'

I've always been a fussy eater. When I was five and I didn't eat my rice, Amma said the policeman down the road would bring his 'big scary dog' to bite me. When I told my girlfriend this story, she cracked up and shook her head. 'These people.'

'I know, they were just winging it,' I replied.

Priya's Sri Lankan Tamil too, so she had no look of judgement, or disdain, or condescending sympathy. Our parents were ruled by fear. Terror, you could say. State terror. Indian Peace Keeping Forces dropping a bomb on your school type of terror.

When I was underweight and wouldn't eat, Amma figured out if she took me to play with the rabbits at Murdoch University and ran with me hand in hand, she could swing around and shovel perfect spheres of rice through my gaping smile.

One time Amma broke a plastic spatula on my forehead cos I kept distracting my sisters from eating their pancakes before school. Even she was surprised.

'Chenturan, I don't eat duck.'

'I want it.'

Amma used to watch me pick the diced onions out of her curry, so she started using onion powder in her cooking. She always gave in to my fussiness. So when I said, 'I want it,' I figured the negotiation would be over.

We weren't allowed to eat meat on Fridays. Technically, as Hindus, we're not allowed to eat meat, period. But it's an eternal relationship we have with God, and all long-term relationships require compromise. So Fridays was when the divine warden came to visit. Hide your meat, your leather shoes, free your slater farms, and don't even think about slapping that mosquito.

When I found out my cousin Pratheep ate Red Rooster on a Friday, I began throwing tantrums. Amma eventually let me eat meat at the school canteen. Out of sight, out of her mind. Later, she'd even buy me KFC. She felt sorry for me because my perpetual fussiness also meant perpetual hunger and embarrassment. My sister told me she spent extra time in the prayer room when she bought meat for me on Fridays. It's like she was counting my calories and burning my sins on the karmic treadmill. Unfortunately, I'll still probably be reincarnated into a Steggles chicken.

When Amma was twelve, she went on a day-long train ride across Sri Lanka to drop her brother at the airport. Her mother packed their lunch inside a banana leaf: fried fish, vegetable curry and rice. They unwrapped the leaf on the train and there were six pieces of fish for the five who came onboard. The kids tried to pounce, but her father grabbed it and contemplated. He handed the extra piece to his wife and said, 'Nine children were in her tummy, now her tummy wants fish.' Amma loves this memory of her father. When I ask her why, she says, 'That memory more touch me.'

In a sea of similar moments, I wonder why some are more vivid. Perhaps if it were duck in that banana leaf, my mum wouldn't have registered it at all. Perhaps she would have recoiled and stared out the window.

'Amma, please.'

'I don't eat duck.'

'Why?'

'I don't eat duck.'

'Why?'

'I don't –'

'Amma!'

'Chenturan.'

'WHY!?'

'BECAUSE I HAD A DUCK.'

My heart breaks.

'You had a duck?'

'We had two ducks.'

'Why didn't you say that? … What happened to the ducks? … Did you eat the ducks?'

'No.'

'How did they die?'

'I don't remember.'

'Did your parents force you to eat them?'

'No!'

Turns out the ducks lived a long and happy life.

But why not just say that straight away?

That's what Amma's like. She doesn't look back. Maybe it's not productive to look back when you move to a new country. Maybe inside that treasure chest of memory, the joys reside beside the traumas.

When my parents made mistakes, we explained their behaviour with a buzzword empathy.

Amma and Appa fought a lot in front of us.

Yeah but, civil war, right?

Appa's got a temper–

Yeah but, he saw Black July.

Appa struggles with–

Yeah but, his mum was a child bride.

Amma's always–

Yeah but, her father and brother were murdered.

One night in 2021, my sister and I were sinking into our parents' couch. We weren't being held hostage by designated family time or a celebratory dinner. This was old school laziness. Just in each other's company, like we had done thousands of times as children. No one reached for their phones, or tried to put on a movie. This used to be every day, when at any moment the lounge could explode into a wrestling match, or a monopoly game, or my dad pretending to be some non-descript monster throwing us around.

My sister started painting my nails, and we played YouTube videos of classic Tamil songs from the eighties and nineties. Amma loved it. She gave a cheeky side glance and then lifted her hands to mime playing the flute. Then she danced. She actually tried really hard, with the precise jabs and kicks and melodramatic expressions of a bharatanatyam dancer. She did it for forty-five minutes. This is someone who pants walking up the stairs every morning. Sometimes we would look up, laugh and film her. She was in her own world, like a toddler playing around adults, at times deeply interested in our attention, but mostly lost in her private dimension.

When she stopped dancing, it all poured out of her. She had deep regrets about not going to university and having a professional career.

My mother is the eighth of nine children. The first five were boys, which meant by the time it came to her education, the family had too many loans to keep her in a lady's college on the mainland.

She changed schools five times during high school. Not only that, but her entire class in the remote island of Neduntheeve had to repeat Grade 10 because their standard was too low for the government exams.

She says the confusion and loneliness of being moved around meant she couldn't focus.

Throughout her youth she excelled in the arts. To this day, she has a photographic memory for song lyrics, but she was made to believe the arts were a frivolous education. She veered towards maths, and excelled. At various times, teachers told her to get an education on the mainland, where her abilities could be nurtured.

When she did make it to Jaffna, a Grade 12 teacher, who had never taught Amma, hassled her father to pull her out of the maths pathway because she was a girl and wouldn't have the aptitude to succeed. After numerous calls, her father took the advice, and my mother did subjects like biology, botany and zoology, which she didn't like. Growing plants and cutting frogs took too long, she said.

Amma eventually did not do well enough to go to university, and while she could have repeated Grade 12, she took a job at a bank for convenience.

Amma always says she's proud of being a stay-at-home mother, but she has deep regret about not having a tertiary education or career. She's often not taken seriously in our household. The children of migrants often infantilise their parents because we have to teach them English, and do their administrative errands, and teach them our social etiquette.

Amma said that it was her own fault her life didn't go the way she wanted, because when she moved schools and was a lonely student, she gravitated towards class clowns who teased a boy of little means for wearing the same yellow shirt. She said it was bad karma. Amma would rather believe it was cosmic justice than believe it was the chaos of being pushed around by external forces.

I'm convinced Amma told us all this because she danced. Creative play allows people to access deeper parts of themselves that they often try to ignore in conscious thought. I think dancing transported my amma, and our enthusiasm created a nurturing environment that raised her self-esteem and allowed her to share her story.

We had a vague sense of her challenges, but to hear it in concrete, specific terms was shattering. It was beautifully humbling, too. Our buzzword empathy did not capture her story.

Amma survived war, and was pushed around by the chaotic winds of other men's plans. She lost her brother and father on the same night, when a bomb landed on a school.

But at that Malaysian restaurant, she was actually thinking about her pet ducks. The ducks she swiped off a table when she was ten because they were bringing dirt into the kitchen. A swipe she vividly regrets, and the reason why she doesn't eat duck to this day.

Emergence

I want to return to the mother I emerged from. To have the non-judgement of a child. To give her space to tell me who she is rather than try to impose my preconceptions.

It's beautiful to be humbled by the mysteries of her memory. The mind-altering truffle oil delivered alright, and not a drop had to be eaten.

Pink skates, autistic limbs

Elena Filipczyk

It arrived with native flowers. A friend heard about Mum's sudden death and had sent a gift to show she was thinking of me.

It was a book about suicide.

I laughed when I opened it. Is this her suggested solution?

Reading the book was too frightening an option in those first few days after 26 August. I glanced over the blurb, studied the author's portrait (did her eyes look sad like mine?), then left the book with the collection of slowly dying flowers threatening to take over my sister's kitchen.

A week later, I got a phone call. We had two weeks to empty Mum's house, they told us. Then they'd change the locks. My sister's eyes widened in disbelief as I shook my head. We didn't even need to speak. How are we going to do this? We live hours away.

The woman on speakerphone kept talking. I pretended to listen as I imagined smashing open the locks. One last thing, the woman said. I'm really sorry for your loss.

As Lock Day approached, our anxiety grew. In desperation, we began to list Mum's furniture online.

$50.

$20.

Free. Pick-up only.

Late that afternoon, a middle-aged man arrived for the dining table. Tall and tanned, his lumbering body filled the entire frame of the front door as he looked around the rapidly emptying townhouse.

'So, who died?' he quipped.

'My mum,' I replied, my eyes avoiding his.

In an instant, the man's entire demeanour shifted as he looked more closely at my face. (How old is she?) He mumbled his apologies awkwardly, then left with his free prize. He looked as old as my dad should've been, I realised.

Somehow, Papa had been gone for ten years already. No matter how sick he got, nothing prepared me to lose him at age sixteen. I had nightmares about his death for years – and that I would lose Mama too. And ten years later, that nightmare had come true. I found myself standing in Mum's townhouse, looking at my childhood toys, and choosing what clothes to cremate her in.

With Lock Day in our heads, we found ourselves giving away the furniture Mum was so proud of. Nothing matters anymore, I reassured myself. The box of my old toys didn't matter.

Neither did my books. It was disturbingly easy to get rid of it all, box by box. Bin. Bin. Donate. Bin. Recycle. Bin.

Dealing with things had become easy; but dealing with people became harder than ever. And from the Suicide Book to Lock Day and the Tall Tanned Man, I realised no one knew how to deal with me, either.

The adult orphan. The girl with no parents. The motherless daughter.

It felt like my status was stamped on my forehead, and there was no escaping the discomfort it stirred in everyone around me. I saw it in the pity of my colleagues' eyes. I heard it in the whispers of my friends' mothers. I felt it in the silent glances of extended family at that depressing first Christmas without Mama.

Months passed, and the offers of homemade meals stopped. Eventually, so did the pity. I was finally alone in my grief, primed to follow its commands. Anxious and impatient, I let grief lead me back to the tangible. Restless, I emptied my shelves and desk drawers. Indifferent, I donated half my wardrobe to charity. Angry, I moved out of my share house and into an empty apartment – alone, with no furniture. I unpacked the essentials, but my books, my music collection and the stacks of my old birthday cards and letters weren't enough to fill a room, let alone an entire apartment. And I had just two dusty boxes left. They were from Mum's.

I emptied them onto my garage floor. There were glowing school reports from every year. There were good behaviour awards. There were countless grade-A assignments and dozens of academic awards. All through school and university, these pieces of paper had meant everything to me. Now, they meant nothing. I hadn't kept them for me. I'd kept them for Mum. They were the only physical proof of my worthiness, yet as I read through them one by one on my garage floor, only anguish churned inside me: did I really make her proud?

She'd said it a million times. She was proud of me. So why didn't I believe her?

I realised now. My body remembered the moments I'd rather forget, memories burned into my subconscious with the branding iron of social humiliation.

I couldn't run, but I tried to the point of exhaustion. Every year, I ran with my inhaler in hand and watched the school lap me in cross-country.

I couldn't dance, but I hoped just one more school session would stop me falling over my feet. In Year 2, I went to my best friend's dance recital and saw my mum's face fill with awe and pride. I swallowed my bitter, jealous tears.

I couldn't swim, but I kept going to lessons. Mum watched me flail uncomfortably in the shallow pool, her eyes sad and concerned. The rest of the group swam confidently up the ranks: Dolphin, Marlin, Shark. I couldn't get past Goldfish. Finally, I was pulled out of swimming lessons.

By high school, my shame was matched with fierce embarrassment. I dreaded PE and sport. I hated being picked last, and cursed the inevitable, embarrassing spectacle of my uncoordinated body. I watched the other teenage girls run and play effortlessly, and yearned for the grace and joy of their movement. I watched the teenage boys, envying their natural speed and strength, and burned with embarrassment when their eyes fell on me as I missed another easy catch.

I hated how my body moved. Too wide. Too slow. Too stupid. And yet, I held onto naive hope that with just a little more practice I could catch that ball, make that hoop, score that goal.

I never did. And no matter how many 'A's I got in English or Geography, it wasn't enough to make up for the shame of my awkward, uncoordinated limbs.

At university, I kept up the charade, dedicating myself to studying while secretly wishing I was more like my sporty peers: the girl who played netball, the boy who surfed, the group that went swimming together. They actually enjoyed it.

In second year, I was paired with a girl for a group assignment. At the library after class, she gushed about her athletic hobbies, then quizzed me about sports, high school and my childhood. After a moment of contemplation, she asked: 'Do you think you try so hard at school because you want to make your mum proud and it's the only way you know how, because you were sick and not good at sports?' I sat there stunned, then replied slowly, 'Oh my god, I think you're right.'

She had read me like a book. Pages I hadn't even come to yet. It took me almost ten more years to get my autism diagnosis, and even longer to realise just how deeply my autistic shame affected me.

Sitting on my garage floor and emptying my academic awards into the recycling bin, I thought of the girl who had looked through my soul at the university library almost a decade before. She was right, I wanted to tell her. But most of all, I wanted to tell Mum.

I'm sorry. I've figured it out: I'm autistic, but I still want to be like everyone else. I want to do cool things with my body.

A few months later, I bought a pair of pink rollerskates and a sunset-coloured helmet.

My empty apartment became a roller rink.

Except I couldn't skate. I could barely stand in my baby-pink skates, my legs splaying like a newborn foal's as I held onto the walls around me. But I kept trying. First, inside, on the forgiving hardwood. Then, months later, in my garage, where the smooth, sloping concrete instantly pulled me to my knees, my body smashing into my neighbours' bikes leaning against the wall, both of them falling on top of me. I kept trying.

Eventually, I graduated from the garage floor to the winding footpaths of my local park, where tight turns and stray gumnuts regularly threw me to the grass. The dog walkers and child-toting parents eyed me curiously. I kept trying.

Finally, I built up the courage to go to the skate park. Avoiding the gazes of a dozen intimidating teenage boys, I strapped on my gear and waited on a bench, watching. Then, it happened.

He was on a skateboard, and not much older than me. He had multiple people filming him and he was waiting for his moment. He knew how much speed he needed and had set up a run-up the length of the skate park. With a running start, he dropped into the steepest quarter pipe and propelled himself through the entire skate park, speeding towards a steep, rising bank met by a dead end: a brick wall with an arched, toddler-sized cut-out. Hurtling towards the wall, he suddenly jumped off his board, launching himself into the air – forwards over the brick wall, his board rolling through the arch underneath him. Flying over the brickwork with his arms flailing and his shirts fluttering in the wind behind him, he almost landed it, but when his feet finally returned to his board, he was off balance. The board slipped out from under him and he crashed back-first into the concrete, the force of his propulsion pushing him into a backwards somersault. Somehow, he made falling beautiful. He was art on a concrete canvas.

On the benches, no one laughed. No one judged. People clapped, congratulating the skater for his attempt. His friends helped him to his feet, slapping his back affectionately. He had literally thrown himself into the path of danger for the pure thrill of it, and he was being applauded for failing. For falling. For trying.

I fell in love with the skate park. My skates became my new prized possessions and the skate park my new sanctuary. I'd stumbled into a vibrant, diverse community of supportive strangers, and their currency was compliments and fist bumps.

One afternoon, a girl I'd just met held my hand to steady me as I tried a new trick. Her kindness struck me, and the warmth of her hand lingered on my skin long after her fingers slipped away from mine.

I landed it.

She cheered for me and encouraged me to try it alone. I fell, and nobody blinked an eye.

Everyone falls at the skate park, another girl told me. It's part of the process.

But at the skate park, there's no time limit to fall short of. No race to lose. No team to be picked last for.

Autistics are invisible at the skate park, I realised. Unless someone can read my mind.

Mum, I'm doing something cool with my body.

beyond the cloth

Charaf Tartoussi

My relationship with *hijab* has not always been complicated. There was a time, which feels like very long ago now, that the square chiffon cloth I'd fold and pin to my undercap was an immovable, visible part of my identity, and just like my mother before me, and her mother before her, I was committed to it. That notion changed in the winter of 2017.

I couldn't tell you exactly which world event triggered it, but I can tell you this: the Melbourne air was cold that night, the kind that turns your nose red and forces you to entertain the idea that it might fall off if it got any colder. My *hijab* was blue: navy with magenta flowers on it. It was my favourite, I liked the way the navy blue framed my face and contrasted with my skin, I thought the flowers dancing on the fabric, connected with vines like hands in a *dabke* line made me seem artistic, fun, approachable. I can tell you that the train was three minutes late. That I was coming back from afternoon clinic, where my patient gifted me a box of chocolates to say thank you. That I was stressed about my exams. That it was Wednesday. That I was wearing a pair of white in-ear earphones and listening to 'Sweater Weather' by The Neighbourhood. That we were between Essendon and Glenbervie on the Craigieburn line. I can tell you that there were a handful of people riding in the same carriage as me, that

I admired the pink ombre dye job on the girl sitting in front of me. That I didn't notice him at first. That I thought he had a kind face. That when he approached me, I thought he might have been looking for an empty seat, or directions, or a friendly conversation.

I can tell you that I was wrong. That he was angry. That he was angry with me, for something that had happened in the world that week. I can tell you that what he did was violent. I can tell you that I do not plan on recounting the events of our encounter, because they pose the risk of detracting from the central point of the story, as trauma does.

You only need to know that the interaction did happen, and that it saw me return to university in the spring with my hair worn down in public for the first time since I was nine.

To say that this was the beginning of my complicated relationship with the article of faith I donned for the best part of fourteen years would be a lie. To tell you that I had been completely secure in that relationship at any point in that time, too, is a lie.

To understand where the complications began and how they came to be, we need to go back to the very beginning; as far back as I can remember, my mother, my grandmother and every woman with any semblance of a presence in my life has worn *hijab*. To them, *hijab* is not only a symbol of faith, it is a practice in closeness to Allah, an identifier of relation to every other Muslim you encounter, and a marker of character that has been interwoven into our identities for generations.

As a child, I would sit beside my mother and watch as she got ready. I'd marvel at the way she'd fold the fabric down the middle so it formed a triangle and place it on her head where it'd fall like a halo, the way she gathered the fabric along the sides of her head and joined the pieces just under her chin with the gold pins she'd gotten on the trip we took to the motherland when I was four. In those moments, my mother's framed face was ethereal and it was her *hijab* that highlighted its beauty, not because of the coloured fabrics she'd choose or the way she styled it, but because this was something that brought her a palpable joy, a sense of peace, and I wanted so much to be a part of that one day.

My mother wanted me to be a part of it, too. On bi-annual Eid trips to the mosque, she would dress me in the smaller *hijabs* she'd have shipped in from Syria. Then she'd dress herself and examine our reflections in the mirror and beam with pride. This was her reaction every time, and then it wasn't anymore.

After the twin towers fell and the news broke of the hijackers who shared in our faith, the world's attitude towards my mother and, in turn, her attitude towards fostering my relationship with *hijab* changed. I remember very few things from that time: my mother crying while she watched the reruns on television, how she struggled to explain the news to us, my grandfather's terminal cancer diagnosis, the birth of my brother, and Tracy.

Tracy was a store attendant at the Dimmeys on Bell Street. My mother would take us to shop there often and Tracy, who worked on the checkout most days, would make polite conversation with her, ask her about the family, and sometimes, just like so many of the other women we'd meet, she would compliment her on her *hijab*. In mid-September of that year, on a trip for school supplies just before the beginning of the school term, Tracy greeted my mother without a smile for the first time. My mother stopped receiving compliments on her headscarves after that.

When, in November of that year, I began entertaining the idea of observing *hijab*, her initial reaction was to tell me to wait until I was a little older. She would tell me this again on my eighth birthday and then again when Ramadan came around. By the time I was nine, I had begun to realise that this was now her established response to my desire, and I became more determined about the matter. On the third day of the Ramadan of my ninth year, I started wearing *hijab* despite her advice and she, begrudgingly, found it in herself to support me.

My observation of *hijab* was relatively comfortable for most of my adolescence; I attended an Islamic school where a white chiffon headscarf was part of the uniform and, as I got older, more and more of my friends began to participate in the practice. By the eighth grade, five out of the seven girls who formed my high-school friendship group wore *hijab*; by the twelfth grade, we all did. The experience of Muslim teenage girlhood is not all that unique; we swapped makeup tips at recess, modified our uniforms to keep up with trends set by our favourite *hijabi* YouTubers, had posters of our favourite singers blu-tacked to the doors of our lockers and read *Dolly* and *Girlfriend* in the parking lot while we waited for our parents. That period of time was idyllic in that way; we weren't constantly confronted with the question of how the way we dressed fit into the wider world we belonged to. That isn't to say that we were unscathed by it, just that instead of being deeply wounded by the western context in which we lived, we merely grazed our knees on its existence.

Emergence

Growing up, my cousin Rana and I were often invited to sleep over at my grandmother's house. One night, after a fit of giggles had faded into the stillness of the early September air, in a voice so soft you might have missed it if you exhaled too loudly, she told me that she sometimes wished she hadn't started wearing *hijab*.

It was the first time anyone had ever shared that sentiment openly, albeit ashamedly, with me.

I lay there in my teddy bear pajamas, and the lopsided bob my mother had given me, at a loss for words. I had never felt so understood. I was in my early teens and trying to figure out who I was going to be, but I couldn't find myself anywhere. Not in magazines or the after-school television shows I'd watch with my siblings, not at the movies or between the pages of my favourite novels, not on a ballot paper, or an ad break. I felt invisible to the world outside my community and, sometimes, I wished I didn't.

In retrospect, that conversation planted the seed of change in me. A seed that would lay dormant until I was much older.

It wasn't until I started attending university that the connection between my *hijab* and I really began to strain. I still wore it every time I left the house, but I had become acutely aware of the way people treated me for it, and that awoke a resentment in me. I would often imagine a reality where I didn't wear *hijab*; a reality with no microaggressions, no curious strangers, no distant colleagues, no awkward FGM tutorials, no racial slurs, no random explosives checks, and no run-ins with James. I was ashamed to admit it back then, but I yearned for that.

James was a larrikin type whom I met on a Wednesday afternoon in my first year of dental school. We had just begun learning about the nervous network of the head and neck when he sat next to me and asked me for a pen. That afternoon, as I sat alone in the student common room, eating my lunch of leftover shakriye from the night before, he took it upon himself to approach me and ask if I had hoped to come to uni that day dressed as the wife of Osama bin Laden. The entire cohort erupted with laughter as all of the heat in my body rushed to my face and stayed there. I was upset, I was angry, but more than anything, I was humiliated.

I went home early that day and filed a complaint with the faculty. When I returned a week later, nothing had changed. I spent the next two years pushing back against James and his relentless bullying, and attempting to maintain my relationship with my *hijab* despite it.

After the unfortunate incident of the winter of my sixth year at uni, my attempting stopped. No matter the state of our relationship, I no longer felt safe wearing my *hijab* in public and, in the end, that was reason enough to stop engaging with the practice after thirteen years of determined commitment to it.

On the first day of classes that spring, I took the Nicholson Street tram, keeping my hands busy with the buttons on my linen blouse. The air on the skin of my neck, my ears, my scalp felt abnormally foreign to me. The woman who had taken the tram with me for the last two years smiled at me for the first time. In class, my peers greeted me with their double takes and their unasked questions. I got compliments on my hair and was told I looked nice that day, more times than I had in the six years preceding it.

Emergence

It was uncomfortable in the way that mourning is when everybody else feels there is cause for celebration in the midst of your loss. I had imagined for so long what it would be like to emerge into the world without the article of faith it had punished me for and, now that I had, the reward left an unpleasant aftertaste.

Five years have passed since that winter night in 2017 saw me wear my *hijab* in public for the last time. Our relationship is less complicated now. I know that hiding is the price I pay for the comfort and safety I have been allowed since then. I know that our relationship will always exist in some capacity, and I know, more than anything, that I still long for a world that can find it in itself to celebrate that.

War/Dance

Dahlia Eissa

At night, I dreamed. My coin-tasselled red sash in my veins, pulsing to the *doom tak tak, doom tak* of my heartbeat. When I woke, I'd touch my body, unsure if what had happened to it was real.

My body. Its worth etched all over my flesh, stamped on every cell.

That was the unspoken, inviolable mantra with which I was raised. Anything immodest, my cleavage, my cunt, was shameful. So my family's Muslim faith was a perfect fit for me, a tortoiseshell in which to hide my body. A woman's best sense of herself was spiritual, cerebral. Fleshy, bodily were trouble. Molested by a boy at the beach when I was eleven, I knew in my gut when I ran away from him not to tell my mother, for fear she would slap me. Not to tell my father, for fear he would stop talking to me.

That disconcerting smear of blood appeared two years prior. So I already had an ample Arab bosom and African ass I desperately tried to starve and purge. And in school, my thick, unruly curls and brown skin stood out in a sea of Olsen twins wearing ankle socks while I, in a feeble attempt to hide my calves, wore socks to my knees. My body didn't fit in, to anything. Mostly, it didn't fit in to the person I believed I had to be – to be respected, safe, loved.

179

Emergence

There were adjacent mantras – get an education, a good job, make money, don't expect a man to take care of you. Mantras many conservative patriarchal families adopt along with a new home country. Where they move into two-storey houses, use the latest appliances, and buy frozen peas. There are some old ways they'll let go of because the new ones look like progress. But there are some they won't shake because those would feel like chaos.

The Arabic word for chaos is *fitna*. It can mean secession, upheaval, trial or temptation. It refers to something frightening, intolerable. Some would add mischief, desire, sex, women's bodies, Eve, Lot's wife, the Queen of Sheba.

Fitna is when women start behaving like men, sometimes. When things get unnatural. When women start to say no, answer back, wear what they want, want sex, don't want kids. But it's OK if they take out the trash, put their pay cheque into a joint account, though they have to pretend not to see the porn their dads hide at the bottom of the dustbin, and not ask their husbands why their savings paid for his new Breitling.

The anomalies are a mind fuck. The duality exhausting. You cannot escape your body. A woman's body is sex, and her mind is morally obligated to reject it. A kind of mind/body fuck.

But the mind can try to escape. And my mind went to war with my gut, creating a fantasy world where my body could be disappeared. Be better, smarter, holier than thou. My collars got higher, my hems lower. I woke before dawn for prayer. Then I started to shower twice, three times a day, recoiling from anyone's touch. If anyone knocked, there was no body here.

Then the war started to have physical feelings. A brittleness to my bones, as though one blow and I'd fall and shatter. A tightness to my skin, as though seams would split open. I was hyper-agitated, one eye open, never at rest. My mind incapable of accepting that all of me would always be trapped in a family that played Whac-A-Mole with any unruly bits of me that dared come out of my tightly prescribed hole.

Eventually the air became dense, as though I was breathing through a thin straw. With each exhale, I felt my lungs collapse, tearing from my ribs. At university, I'd be in the middle of a class and have to collect my things and leave. Driving to work, I'd have to pull over because I couldn't see through the mist over my eyes. In the shower, I'd end up on my hands and knees crying and crying as though my body was trying to exorcise a grief within me, aching for the water to wash it all away. When I woke in the morning, I'd pull the covers over my face, desperate to fall back asleep.

A face and body so sullen are discomfiting. My family was angry, embarrassed, confused. It was unladylike to be so displeasing. Un-Egyptian to be so inhospitable.

Our family doctor did not hide his animus towards my family. He told me he'd help me. Then told me to get my degree and get the fuck out of there.

My shell cracked wide open when I moved, fled, first to Boston, then to New York. If there's a place in the world where every body moves to their own groove, it's New York City. No one watching. No one judging. And I started to think the God I really wanted to believe in, of unconditional love and compassion, wouldn't give a shit about the length of my skirt. That was a man-made God talking, controlling, subjugating.

That revelation, revolution, cannot be understated. My self and body merged, living out loud. I became one of those people to whom others gravitate. Keep to yourself your aphorisms about beauty being on the inside. Beauty on the outside is power. It not only transforms you, it transforms the world around you. The cab halts to a stop. Your drinks are on the house. People do not step in front of you unless they're opening the door for you.

My family had no idea what I got up to. I figured it served them right. But I knew even though I'd gone to Harvard on two scholarships and paid my own rent in one of the toughest cities in the world, I was still a girl until a man fucked me. That fact deserves to be stated as crudely as it is the truth. A virginal body is a girl's body, until her cunt is penetrated and she's transformed. That's why we're not allowed to wear tampons. I always looked for signs on a newlywed, like before and after photos. What about her now makes her a woman?

A wedding night is momentous – *leilat el dukhla* – the night of entering – the woman, married life, the marital home. Once her husband pierces that membrane (or pushes past it if she's pliable – which might make him ask questions), she loses her virginity, and gains competency as a woman. In that second. That's all it takes. Is it something that happens to her body? Her mind? Her spirit? If she likes what's happening to her, nitric oxide will expand her blood vessels, pumping warm crimson to her lips – all six of them. She'll get wet and swell. Nipples harden, sensitive to touch. Pulse, pressure, dopamine, epinephrine, all rising. Is that what makes a woman? But what if none of that happens? What if the sex sucks? Is it just the sex? Or with those drops of blood that may stain the sheets is there a shedding of girlhood?

Or is it all in her head? In everyone's head?

My body a million miles away didn't care so much, but every now and then my mind would wonder. Trying to unpack their world. Still hoping that one day ...

At an Arabic dance party, I bought a coin-tasselled red sash. My parents had video tapes of Egyptian belly dancers. Dancing was something watched. OK for others. Seriousness was correct. Playfulness was not. But in New York I would head to Midtown after work to Nourhan's studio. Taking off my coat, she'd pull up my shirt and tie a knot at the back, exposing my midriff. Then push down my skirt and tie my sash low on my hips. Tareq would play the *tabla* for us. 'Aliyah, he called his instrument – exalted, from heaven, sublime – because he believed she made the sounds of happy feet dancing, the sound of pure excitement, pounding on the marble floors of heaven.

A deep bass *doom* – with his right hand, he'd strike the centre of her taut skin, then lift his hand to open the sound. I'd raise my heels and start to pound – *doom tak tak, doom tak, doom tak tak, doom tak*. Chin up, shoulders back, I'd snake my arms and shimmy my thighs, and submit to 'Aliyah. The *doom tak tak, doom tak* resetting the rhythm of my heart. Instead of the *thump thump thump* of what am I doing, what am I saying, how do I look, I'd pound away self-consciousness. No need to spy on myself from afar, hear myself as others do, keep myself in check, correct my every move. The prickly on the outside smoothed away. The agitation on the inside gone. I'd sweat out sadness and fear, and submit my mind and body, in a way I couldn't do five times a day facing Mecca. Five times a day, I tried and failed. Finally, I met God. I danced with God. My feet happy, pounding on the marble floors of heaven. And I'd forget. Untether my mind from them.

But then my body got sick.

Scleroderma. A chronic, disabling auto-immune disease that destroys connective tissue.

At times the decline was steady. Clawing my fingers so I could no longer clap my zills. Tightening my skin so my arms could no longer undulate like rippling water. Scarring my lungs so I had no breath to twirl and twirl. Wasting away the fat in the soles of my feet so if I'd pound, I'd pound on bone. Piggybacking is Raynaud's phenomenon. The attacks feel like my extremities are stuck to an iced metal pole. So I'd cover my midriff, and my hands and feet, to stay warm.

I tried everything – chemotherapy, Ayurveda, meditation. But illness and deformity shrunk my world. My gravitational pull became a repellent. People avoided eye contact. Men stopped flirting. The urge to shroud my unfit body returned. Nothing but trouble, back in my shell. My self and body separated again. My body hating my self for wasting all that time. I should have run away sooner. I could have become a dancer. My self hating my body for not giving it enough time. I'd just started to like me.

At times the decline was a Mach 3 nosedive.

Blood pressure dropping, heart rate rising, unbearable excruciating pain that felt like Bloods and Crips knifing it out in my belly, then yelling, 'She's dying. She won't make it. ICU needs to make room for her NOW!'

Stripped bare on an operating table, my belly carved open, hands digging deep, taking out my entrails, inspecting what would kill my body, what would keep it alive. Four days later, I woke up in ICU, a puddle of jelly from muscle and nerve atrophy, with sixty per cent of my intestines removed. Ischemic. Dead. I spent twenty-one days in recovery, fighting pain, infections, pneumonia. Everything tasted like metal. Eating was exhausting. Down to thirty-seven kilograms, my bones skewers threatening to pierce through emaciated flesh. My hair falling out in clumps. For the first time without guilt, I drank whole milk and put sugar in my tea. A physiotherapist came twice a day to teach me how to breathe properly again, how to swallow, sit up on the side of the bed without falling off. Reacquainting my self with every part of my body I needed to survive.

I would touch. Blue veins bulging from blood clots. Scabs from IV lines that had been stitched to my groin. Pressure wounds raw, weeping. My self found an intimacy with them. Found compassion. There was still time.

The exit to the hospital had a revolving door. Stepping out onto the sidewalk, I put my hand on my belly, stroking the long, puckered scar from plexus to pubis. Taut like the skin of 'Aliyah. *Doom tak tak, doom tak.* There had to be a new way to dance.

Scarred and stronger

Saneia Norton

The Hungarian is in a mood today. Radiotherapy is so boring, so inconvenient, so depressing. And he's missing my sister. Her massed curls, almond eyes and long legs made an impact in the crowded bunker.

'Where is Shirley Temple?'

'I drove myself today.'

He leans close. 'Tell me, is her personality as wild as her hair?'

Pissed off and protective, I withdraw to the other side of the room.

Cold air on my bare chest. Technicians push and pull my torso, conversing in millimetres. Their rulers and markers highlight my tattoos and position the bed to exact coordinates. A cheery 'Here we go!' and they leave. I lie still in the semi-dark. The bulky machine revolves through three different angles with a series of whirrs, beeps and clunks. Any movement could expose my internal organs to radiation. I take shallow breaths and stare at the ceiling, where a fellow patient has taped a picture of lambs in red neckerchiefs.

———

The last night at work before surgery. Kind words unhinge my careful exit plan.

'Are you going to be OK?'

'I don't know.'

'When will we see you again?'

'I don't know.'

I'm leaving the biggest project of my career. Meetings, milestones, deliverables and deadlines crowd my mind. Eighty-hour weeks keep me a step ahead of jeering project managers and calcified engineers. Eighteen months of hard slog. One hundred meticulous drawings. Five million dollars. We're about to go into construction and I've bought a neon-green tape measure to keep the builders in line. My boss is impressed, but I'm running on Cokes and adrenalin. I down beers and talk shit with my team. At home, James keeps dinner warm but I'm too drunk to eat.

There's no letting go. My project, my identity and my old life are ripped away with my fingernails still attached and I'm left gasping in blackness.

———

Three scars on my chest. A display of surgical skill: genius, rockstar and cowboy. The genius spoke in medical mutterings. 'Seventy to eighty per cent success rate these days ... we'll move the flesh around ... take a bit more margin ...' Ten years on, the ultrasound technician scans muscle layers for the surgical cut and nearly gives up – a hairline on the screen. Rockstar surgeons have megawatt grins and expensive suits. They flirt with the nurses and send ripples down the corridors. Watch out for the cowboys though. The last surgeon barely meets my eyes before putting me under. His ugly, rough-handed stitches leave me teary.

———

My breast care nurse is sympathetic then suddenly brutal: 'Thirty-seven with no kids? You'll want to freeze some eggs before chemo. Better get on that.' Shocked and stressed, we squeeze in a rushed cycle, discovering that I'm low on eggs and James has weak sperm. My rage finds focus. I scream silent obscenities at chatty nurses. Seethe at power suits fitting in appointments before work. Save special scorn for those with toddlers coming in for a second baby. Emptied of empathy and three feeble eggs, I lock the experience away and face forward for chemo.

———

Midnight on a Friday and emergency is in full swing. Ambos, drunks and broken bones. I'm at the nadir, the point when the chemo drugs have decimated my white blood cells and I can't fight infection. Temperature 38.2 degrees. My bald head and chemo-card get me to the front of the queue. Bloods, chest x-ray, urine test. The pregnant nurse comes to collect my sample and recoils when she sees the cytotoxic sticker. My bodily fluids could harm her unborn baby. Another nurse takes her place. The cute doctor with the Slavic accent tells me the drugs have scarred my median cubital vein.

———

Drenched sheets. My body on fire from the inside out. It starts with warning pinpricks of heat then sweeps from scalp to toes. I push away from James, yell 'Flushing!' and fling off the covers. Sweat pours out of me. Blood rushes in my ears. I search for a cool spot on the pillow. After it passes, we resume our spoon. His body heat will set me off again, but I don't care. I'm sore, numb, swollen, but I need his hands on me. Desperate to feel normal. Does he still even want to have sex? Will he leave if we can't have kids? Worrying towards dawn ... how many years do I have? The online forums are heartbreaking, terrifying. I can't find community with dying people.

———

My new life has a kind of peace. Days spent in front of the telly. I'm an expert in Korean pop music circa 2011. I sit in the garden and look at grass blades. I live for gossip and glimpses of outside life – comedic kids, a new crush, workplace dramas. I lose my taste for caffeine and return to the comfort of cold Milo.

Only five people see me bald. Experiments with scarves, hats, bandannas. I buy ten wigs and end up wearing the cheapest. Leave it squashed and unwashed on the bedroom floor like a sleeping ferret. I won't need it when my hair comes back. Combined with a baseball cap and glasses, I pass for a healthy person. They'd never know.

I need to get in water but the beach feels too rough, scratchy, exposed. A friend has a black-tiled magnesium pool. Solo, I duck under and push off from the wall. Spear through silky water like a torpedo. My lumpen body weightless.

I join an exercise class for eighty-year-olds. They ask if I can plug in my phone and play 'some of that young people's music'. I don't think they're ready for K-pop. I choose my Motown soul playlist and watch them relax and smile. We groove to Marvin Gaye, Aretha, and the Four Tops.

Crying on the loo. Severely constipated by the anti-nausea meds. My chemo nurse recommends eight sachets of Movicol in a litre of water. 'Eight?' I repeat the instruction to be sure. Violent explosions. More tears, but I'm already crafting a story I'll dine out on for years. The procedural question: 'Have you opened your bowels today?' A check box can't capture the primal agony.

Lurid scenes imprinted on smooth, white tiles. Midnights in the mirror with light bouncing off my head. Technicolor urine and toxic waste. Peeling off wound dressings and wiping away pubic hair. The gut punch of the final, failed pregnancy.

———

These last few weeks have been all about hair. Obsessed. Nose pressed to the bathroom mirror, heat lamp on for maximum visibility, I track the progress of lashes and eyebrows. On each brow bone, a grey shadow appears beneath the skin. I see the tiny, tiny hairs long before James does and pester him relentlessly. 'Can you see them now?'

Noses touching. Intense squinting.
'How about this angle? Anything?'
Finally, 'Yes! I see them!'

We jump around like maniacs, whooping, hugging, invincible.

Dear Ma, with love

Grace Huang

How do I explain to you, Ma, who I used to be, who I am now, who I am becoming?

How do I explain?

That I was so scared what you would say, when I came home that night in too-large sick bay trousers. 'What happen to your pant?' Angry hands clasping my thin shoulders. I got pushed into a puddle, but he couldn't see me, it was just an accident, Ma. I'm sorry, please don't be mad. What kind of school was this, that this could happen to her daughter? That when you stormed into the school office and demanded that the kid say sorry, I watched in quiet awe as my mother's form rose up, my warrior and protector.

That I was so envious of that dark-haired girl with the gold earrings, whose poster, 'Trains', was stuck so proudly on the class-room wall, bright with colours and sequins, each letter precise, each paddle-pop stick glued neatly in place. The night before, I had pleaded tearfully, fearfully, for your help, and you, finally home after your long day at the chemicals factory, could only heave a sigh.

'Gracie, why you always leave to last minute?' My 'poster' – a hasty wad of A4 pages on the Boeing 747, black and white (we had to save the colour) – stapled to the bottom left corner of the wall, an afterthought.

How do I explain?

That feeling – a gnawing, slow burn – when I chanced upon the picture of that dark-skinned boy from Lesotho, sorting through our discarded things, the river behind him dyed denim blue. Something died in me then, but in its place was planted a small seed, nestled in among the burning.

You'd left your job at the factory years ago. With my sister born, we needed a bigger house, a bigger life, so you bought a furniture shop out in Auburn, the streets there lined with charcoal chicken and Lebanese bread. Bold red lettering pronounced its name to the world: 'BIG SAVINGS' (yes, actually). It had the added bonus of being close to my tuition college. I spent slow Saturdays solving for 'x' in that small room out back, timber and flat packs crowded around me: 'Teak', 'King single', 'Fragile – handle with care'.

How do I explain?

That after I got the marks you wanted, I finally had space to dream – about that boy and his river, about a different kind of world, a gentle, mindful world. That I loved language, loved the wilds, but I also loved you – and the future you saw for me with those weary eyes was 'professional, you know, better than me and your father'. And so law school it was, but with Chinese and Latin for interest.

That I was the only Asian in the whole Classics department. That everyone there seemed to come from anywhere but here – Mosman, Manly, Glebe, Woollahra. That every time someone asked me where I lived, I had to explain – 'Oh, way out west; you know, between Parramatta and Castle Hill?', the question mark lingering above us. That after stalking the shimmering streets all summer, slipping resume after resume over shopfront counters, I arrived at my first day of LATN3601 Ovid's *Metamorphoses* to this: 'So we stayed at Val D'Isere', 'Oh, isn't it just gorgeous out there?', 'Absolutely stunning, you should come with us next time!' You had always hated the snow, we Cantonese don't like the cold.

How do I explain?

How exhilarating it was to step up onto those upturned milk crates, our makeshift stage, introducing our speaker for the night. It was our first campaign, and under the fairy lights of that curry house attic, I took in the sea of earnest faces before me – seeing that same anger, injustice, urgency and hope reflected in the mirrors of their eyes. From that seed had emerged a small sprout. It hesitated, reaching for warmth, nourishment. You would have been floored if you'd seen me up there (but you didn't – Thursdays were Late Night). You always thought I was the quiet one, the dutiful big sister. That night, I shed another skin – my younger self, shy, quiet, died another death.

How electric it was to sit in that seminar room every Monday afternoon, learning of the tools we lawyers had at our disposal to build something better, to shift power from those who currently held it. Law reform, strategic litigation, lobbying, media campaigns, grassroots organising – these concepts reverberated through my mind, intoxicated by an imagined future.

How do I explain?

That I wept, as I filled out form after form. 'Why do you want to work for our firm?', 'What interests you about commercial law?', 'What makes you a cultural fit at our firm?' That I knew you wanted to help so badly, but the most you could do was leave those orange pieces, carefully segmented, in a bowl outside my closed door as a silent offering.

That when I graduated after five years' full-time study with no grad contract, no job, no prospects, I thought I had failed – not only myself, but also you, Ma, and that hurt the most.

How do I explain?

That somehow, in the two years since, I survived, I healed, and now I am blooming. I am learning the language of our trees, our rivers, our mountains and, with it, the words we use to cut them down, take their water, mine beneath their depths. I am learning to cut those thick, invisible ropes that bind the hands of our people to the bottom rung. I am building a peaceful revolution.

That I am perched on the threshold, new wings half-spread, hesitating. I am taking one last look at the home you made for us, furniture mismatched (sourced from Lao Zhang, our supplier), a print of Tinkerbell displayed proudly on the wall above our family photos, 'Create your own magic'. Now I have to choose. What will I take with me, what will I leave behind?

That I am no longer that child you protected all those years before. That what was first seed, then sprout, is now in full blossom, glowing red in the September sun.

Sometimes you muse to me that you wish you learned tax law or strata law so you could manage your investments better. Not having enough all those years, you learned to get a kick out of getting a return.

You dream about understanding this alien world of statutes, by-laws and exceptions. I dream about a world that is yet to be born.

How do I explain, Ma, that 'success' to me looks like dappled light, books on a shelf, a gentle home – not investment properties, European holidays, dinners in the penthouse? How do I explain that I want to live slow, live small, tread lightly upon this earth?

How do I explain, Ma, that I have died again and again to arrive here today, fierce, heart open, skin raw as a newborn's?

How do I explain, Ma, that I am finally emerging – emerging from our sleepy suburban cocoon that has been my shelter and my training ground all these twenty-four years. That the world is my world, that this is my journey and a great big adventure awaits me, that I have to go, that you have to let me go?

How do I explain?

Smiley

Sangeetha Jesudason

The relationship between a patient and their doctor is sacred, they tell you when you start. This unwell, fragile person gazes into the wise bearded face of this tall White man, and immediately feels bathed in a calm golden glow. They relax, safe in the certainty that they will be well cared for.

The relationship between a patient and their junior doctor, however, is rather different. Their first reaction is usually disappointment; they came here specifically for answers, for expertise, and here, instead, was this sweaty, terrified twenty-four-year-old, shaky handed and holding a rather large needle. The second reaction is pity; they find themselves feeling oddly sorry for this human-shaped cloud of anxiety – oddly protective. The third, if we're lucky, is a sort of intimacy borne of desperation and mutual powerlessness.

The most important thing to remember, though, is that this intimacy isn't … real. We never really know you, or you, us, but it feels nice to have a confidante. A person who learns the colour of your sputum, the origin of your every scar, the darkest secrets of your body, but may not know your middle name. We're somehow equal parts perfect strangers and best friends.

And that's what Robbie was. He was my friend. Over three years, we gathered enough fragments to eventually build a whole relationship. He knew when I got dumped, I knew when his daughter stopped talking to him. I rejoiced when his first round of chemo was over, and sat with him while he joked, barely covering the most profound despair, about not wanting to do this anymore. A fun, casual banter built on years of genuine respect and affection.

He made me the doctor I am today, just by being kinder than necessary to someone who needed it.

———

It's 3.30 on a Monday afternoon. Time has completely ground to a halt; there were twenty-one new admissions over the weekend. As lowly interns, my job and Cam's job is to scurry around and play yet another titillating round of Where The Hell Are The Notes Today (in their respectively labelled pigeonholes? No, of course not, that would be much too easy), and then try and scribble plans that we don't understand, in handwriting that no one else can understand. We take turns presenting patient information. Even my consultant, the usually chatty and delightful Dr Lister, is becoming increasingly short, trying not to lapse into a standing coma. We've finally hit the last two patients.

'And now, we've got old mate Chunky! Chunky is a fifty-eight-year-old male, admitted from emergency with infected diabetic ulcers, which are recurrent and have previously required amputation. Non-compliant with insulin, end-stage renal failure. How ya doing, Chunk!'

I am vaguely horrified by the fact that my co-intern Cam seems to have just fat-shamed an actual human patient to their actual human face, although no one else seems to be batting an eyelid.

Cam has a rare gift for instantly reading a room and blending in seamlessly, and I truly hate him for it. We both started together as interns four weeks ago, and after six years of flop sweat and imposter syndrome, I was decidedly, woefully average. Haven't killed anyone, but my boss definitely asked if I was the new medical student last week. Cam, on the other hand, seems like he's been doing this for years, despite equally knowing fuck all about what it means to be a doctor. I'm far too full of jealousy to be impartial though; he could rescue and rehome one-legged puppies as a side hustle, and I'd STILL think he was a complete and utter fuckweasel.

'Chunky, we talked about this. If you don't use your insulin, you'll keep getting infections, and we're going to have to take the rest of that foot. Is that really what you want?' My consultant is both unimpressed and utterly unsurprised.

Oh. So we're all calling him Chunky now. Cool cool cool, that seems totally appropriate. I feel deeply uncomfortable about this, but hell, I've felt uncomfortable since I got here. It's like I've been given a gorgeous, expensive dress in an unflattering, scratchy fabric that also happens to be two sizes too small. I wear my doctoring clumsily, certain that everyone can see my intellectual backfat. I spend an inordinate amount of time thinking about irrelevant things, such as whether this is a name he really chose for himself, or if this is how he's survived in the world as a big man, taking the power back from his haters.

'Fuck it, I'll get a cane. Better'n jabbin meself in the arse all day long, I'll tell ya that for free!'

He spies me standing in the corner, trying desperately to look wise.

'MISS INDIA! Look at your gorgeous eyes! Will you marry me?'

He stands up and opens his arms expansively, a gentle fart-breeze accosting the remainder of the four-bed bay. His gown hangs open at the back, giving us a prime view of his posterior real estate.

'You couldn't afford the number of cows I'm worth, Chunky.'

It wasn't a particularly funny joke, but the room exploded; from behind the next curtain, a glorious horse-guffaw. 'HA. She told you, Chunk! That's my girl!'

That was when I met Robbie.

'Robert Prentice is a sixty-four-year-old man who presented with shortness of breath. His wife found him, um, sorry, his wife noticed he was wheezy at breakfast and ...'

My storytelling prowess is decidedly not welcome on this already interminable round. It would be years before I learned to give a snappy handover, a skill Assface Cam has already mastered. I hate him, I hate him, I hate him.

'He ... um.' I look over at my registrar, pleading.

'All good, Sana. Mr Prentice presented with a week's worth of shortness of breath and splenomegaly, full blood count revealed an inexplicable anaemia. His blood film indicated non-Hodgkin's lymphoma; we're waiting on haematology to review. We've transfused him.'

'Good. Robert, I'm Dr Lister, I was on call last weekend. We'll do the basic things, but we'll be handing your care over to Dr Nadkarni, the oncology doctor, so that they can look after your cancer. Any questions for us?'

'Does this mean that Smiley over there won't be my doctor? I like her, she's got some sass!'

'Haha, well, as it happens, Smiley's one of the ward interns, so you'll see plenty of her.'

For the first time in four weeks, I feel like I belong.

———

'Robbie, you know you're my favourite patient, but what have I told you about following me around the hospital? Lyn, did you condone this nonsense behaviour?'

'Morning, Smiley! Not my fault. Couldn't find another good doc in the joint, could I, Lyn?'

'Excuse me, she was talking to me. Now shut it and breathe, stupid!'

Lyndal was Robbie's wife, and I was obsessed with them. Their marriage was the most wonderful manifestation of long-haul love that I'd seen in a long time. A practical, kind and gorgeous love. A love full of humour and warmth. A love full of jokes about resurrecting him and killing him herself, if he dared to die on her. For the three years I'd known him, he'd been in and out of various parts of the hospital, veering wildly between states of unwellness, from mild to desperate. For all those three years, Lyn gave him stability, strength and sarcasm, and most importantly, a sense of normalcy.

I turned to face the cast of thousands that made up a Monday morning ward round in the ICU.

'Robert Prentice, sixty-seven-year-old male, day two of admission for respiratory failure on a background of NHL, recent bleomycin and radiation therapy. Provisional diagnosis of pneumonia, for which he is on pip-taz and vancomycin, but our differential, of course, is BILI. Rapid deterioration on the ward, requiring BiPAP, currently 50% oxygen and pressures of 18 on 8.'

Robert's oncology team had admitted him two days before from Emergency, and over 12 hours, he deteriorated dramatically. He was one step away from a mechanical ventilator, and no one wanted to take that step. BILI certainly sounded kind of cute, like a pet guinea pig, but it was actually a dangerous form of lung damage, caused by one of his chemo drugs. We do this sometimes, come up with adorable acronyms to describe terrifying things. BOOP, VILI, ZEEP; was this an ICU or a Marvel comic, am I right? Is this thing on?

I'd admitted him over the weekend, made that truly hysterical BOOP, VILI, ZEEP joke and laughed about how he looked particularly handsome under the spaceman mask. I'd put a fiddly large cannula in his jugular vein and started some medications to help his heart. Cue delightful banter between Lyn and Robbie about how she'd like to be the one stabbing him in the neck, cue laughter and subsequent admonishment to STAY STILL, MATE, THIS IS A GIANT NEEDLE.

All of this chit-chat was a kindness, a pretend casualness barely disguising an all-encompassing dread. A dread that the mask wouldn't work, and that I would have to intubate him: a life-or-death gamble, with his level of lung damage. I hated to admit this, but really, it was a dread, selfish and pathetic, that I'd have to be the one to let him go.

I watched him like a hawk, and when he started breathing easier, so did I. Hope is not a good colour on critical care doctors, though I didn't know that at the time. Just one of many lessons I was yet to learn.

They did not call me when he died. I found out three months later, in an irritatingly casual conversation with my boss. I was furious that no one had told me, but then, I don't know if anyone knew how much he meant to me. I don't know if he knew how much he meant to me.

See, in the beginning, the only thing you have to prove you belong is a piece of paper. You cling to your little MBBS like a pathetic barnacle, completely susceptible to every mean egotist medic, every asshole radiologist, every bitchy scrub nurse. The resident punching bag for every insecure small human to smack around whenever they felt powerless. Robbie was kind to me when there was absolutely nothing to gain from it. He made the conscious decision to uplift a slightly wretched, constantly terrified little person, displaying great intuition and empathy. Every time I saw him, it felt like walking into a party full of strangers and seeing your best friend there: an overwhelming sense of relief that, contrary to popular belief, you weren't completely alone.

————

'Just comin' round ya there, mate!'

It's been five years since Robbie died.

I'm sauntering down the hallway of a lovely regional hospital, lecturing a medical student en route to seeing a very sick little chap in Emergency. I'm exclusively a children's doctor now, and I'm a far, far cry from the vomitty, perpetually terrified intern I used to be. As it turns out, the only antidote to this constant, gnawing feeling of inadequacy is, well, becoming adequate. After my years in paediatric intensive care, I am a splendidly capable one-woman resuscitation machine, and there is not much that truly scares me anymore.

'So sorry, let me get out of your way!'

'Haha, don't ya worry there, Smiley!'

It momentarily takes my breath away; no one has called me that in a long time.

I think about how proud he'd be of me. No longer afraid of everything, no longer letting every over-gelled, overconfident twat intimidate me, no longer paralysed by insecurity and indecision. I think about how, thanks to people like him, I grew into the kind of doctor he'd always seen in me, someone competent and kind. And yes, still smiley.

I turn to look at the ward assistant pushing the bed behind me, patiently waiting for me to move, and grin widely.

'Smiley ... ya know what, I think I like that.'

Leaving home

Nadia Mahjouri

It's 1980 and I'm four years old. The garden at our new house sprawls across a suburban hillside, air heavy with the damp scent of wet grass, daphne and morning dew. Restless and searching, my small hands dig through rotting leaf litter, uncovering narrow pathways of patterned bricks that loop and twist towards destinations pre-imagined by long ago gardeners – a magic circle, a fairy ring, a weeping cherry dropping blossoms.

Before I am grown, I will live whole lives in this garden, imagine husbands and princes, and weddings with snowdrop fairies as my bridesmaids and flitter bugs as the orchestra. I will dance under twisted branches of wisteria, lose myself in my waking dreams, sweep floors of petals, sing leaf babies to sleep in their wood-bark beds. I will be the mummy, the daddy, the baby, the sister and the brother, each in turn, all me.

When we first moved in, my mummy set up my cast-iron bed in a room with swirling pink roses on the carpet – my own room, because I am a big girl now. My own room in our new old house, tall walls reaching to a rose in the centre of the ceiling. The light that hangs from it reminds me of a single solid raindrop, a giant frozen tear refusing to fall.

Across the hall is Mummy's room. But for the first time, she is sharing it with someone that isn't me. My heart has happy bubbles, because now it's not just Mum and me. We are a real family now. Mum, me and a Man. Just like the books and the movies and the families of my friends. Two parents.

'Mummy, whose room is this?'

'It's my room, darling. Mine and Geoff's.'

I am excited. I like Geoff, and Mummy is happy. She loves our new house on the hill, just down the road from the primary school, and just up the road from the milk bar.

I climb on her bed. 'Geoff is my new daddy,' I proclaim. 'I'm going to call him Dad from now on.'

But when I look up at Mummy, she isn't smiling. She looks kind of cross, and kind of sad and kind of scared. I don't know why. She looks me in the eye.

'No,' she tells me. 'You can't call him Dad. He's not your father.'

Something changes colour in my insides. 'So, what should I call him?' I ask.

'You call him Geoff. OK. Just Geoff.'

'OK.'

I know Geoff isn't my real father, by the way. I just thought maybe I could call him that since I don't know where my real father is. My real father comes from Somewhere Else. That's what Mum told me. That's why my skin's a different colour to hers and Geoff's and all the other kids at preschool. I wonder where my real father is. And why he doesn't come back.

———

By the time I am a teenager, my mother and I have settled into a conspiracy of silence. We leave each other be – me pretending

I haven't noticed the colour of my skin, her pretending she can't smell the cigarettes on my high school blazer. It works for both of us, pretending the hard things don't exist. While my friends are sneaking out of their bedroom windows, and lying about sleepovers at other people's houses, I never have to bother with such deception. I never lie, because my mother never asks where I am going, or with whom.

Instead, I nod to her as I walk out the door, dressed in jeans, Doc Marten boots and a black jacket, lips painted red. 'I'm going out tonight.'

And she quietly, nervously, asks me, 'Do you have enough money for a taxi home?', which I always do, thanks to my part-time job at Sizzler. I never ask for help, she never asks for information. That's the way we are. Love is plentiful, but questions are not welcome, difficult conversations never had. Time and time again, I watch my mother choose silence over conflict, ignoring issues rather than confronting them, preferring uncomfortable peace over the potential resolution to be gained from difficult conversation.

But Geoff and I make no such agreement. We start to argue, adolescent me pushing against his futile attempts to get me to clean up after myself, to turn the lights off after I leave a room. Stressed, my mother stands in the middle, desperate to smooth the waters, constantly navigating her way between us, wordlessly begging us to get along.

Not that I've been a particularly difficult child. In spite of the silence, or perhaps because of it, I work hard, tirelessly, enthusiastically, to please. An only child, a chocolate-skinned girl being raised by her porcelain-skinned blonde mother and her freckled ginger stepfather, my place in the world has never felt effortless. And so, I try hard to impress – Geoff, my mother, my friends, teachers, coaches. But, when it comes to choosing a direction, a path, I am lost. They all look the same to me, tangled and fraught. I have no idea what I like, who I am.

In Year 12, I seek the advice of the careers counsellor. In a dark office, the middle-aged woman in a blue blouse looks over my report card, my list of achievements, and tells me, 'Well, looking at this, you can do whatever you want!' She laughs. 'I'd go as far as to say – the world is your oyster. All going well, you should have your choice of courses at university. So, what will it be – medicine or law?'

It feels like a trick question.

I think of the time I fainted while looking at a photo of a car crash, my skin clammy and my stomach turning. Dissecting a frog made me vomit. I do not want to be a doctor. I have no interest in the law, but I put it down as number one on my preference list. Melbourne, Sydney, Adelaide. Anywhere but here.

In the end, I enrol at the University of Adelaide. Not for the course, the campus, or the culture in the city of churches. I move for love. In my last year at school, I fell in love with a beautiful blue-eyed, dark-haired man, whose long dreadlocks each finished with a perfect blond curl. Like me, he had grown up in small-town Tasmania, but now he lived in Adelaide, lured there by friends and the promise of decriminalised weed.

And so, in the heat of late January, Mum and Geoff help as I pack up my red Leyland Mini, the back seat packed tight with the contents of my bedroom, my books, my sun and moon bedspread, my plastic sunflowers in a terracotta pot.

The heat of the highway sends a constant hot gust of tarmac-scented air through the rip in the leather by the gearstick. Without Mum, Geoff and I drive across the desert towards South Australia, the whole car shaking as we are overtaken by road trains many times our size, our car smaller than their wheel hubs. We stop overnight in a roadside motel in a town called Nhill, drinking cold beer in the shade after cooling off in the kidney-shaped pool that smells thick with chlorine.

The next afternoon, we arrive at the dirty share house at the base of the Adelaide Hills, and Geoff takes a deep breath as he parks the car in the steep driveway, sweat beading on his bald, freckled head. I try to contain my excitement as he pulls on the handbrake. I run to the door, my long, dark legs hit by the warm sun, the scent of the gum trees in the air. I kiss my boyfriend languidly, passionately, and Geoff, embarrassed, looks away. Inside the rental home, with the torn brown couch and the vodka bottles re-purposed as candle holders, thick wax coating them like a fungal bloom, the boys have tidied away the bongs and the takeaway containers in preparation for our arrival. It is as clean as I will ever see it.

This is the beginning of my life, and my body hums with eagerness, anticipation. I am in such a state, eyes glistening with the promise of a grown-up life, of lipstick and sex, and takeaway noodles from corner-shop hawkers' stands, that I don't notice that Geoff has started to cry. I look up at him as he pulls the contents of my childhood bedroom from the back of the red

Mini, and notice the tears running down his cheeks, his freckled face wet.

'Are you OK?' I ask him. I have never seen him cry before, never seen any real emotion from him. He's just Geoff, always there, not my real dad, but always there, nonetheless.

'Don't you care?' he says, his back against the hot car, heat from the concrete driveway making the light dance in waves around us. 'It just won't be the same at home without you.' His voice breaks and, in that moment, I see, for the first time, the size of his love, the space I occupy in his life, the only child he will ever raise. My father, in every sense of the word but one. I hug him, and feel my excitement turn to guilt and back again.

The taxi pulls up, blocking the narrow road, and beeps.

'That's me.' He wipes his face with the back of his freckled hand. I reach towards him and kiss his cheek.

'Bye,' I say, trying not to seem too eager. 'Hope your flight home is OK. I'll call you tonight.'

We watch as he climbs into the white taxi, placing his small backpack on his knee. I wave goodbye as my boyfriend wraps his arm around my waist and pulls me closer. We walk inside, where a guy called Rick is packing a bucket bong, retrieved from its hiding place behind the couch. He looks up at me.

'Who was that?' he asks. 'Was that your dad?'

I falter, missing a beat, before I smile at him, and reply, 'Yeah. That's my dad. His name is Geoff.'

You (don't) know who I am

Allanah Hunt

There is a sign on the off-white wall with a generic saying, something like *It costs nothing to be kind.* I can hear strains of music through the swinging doors of the theatre, a throwback Maroon 5 song, I think. The bitter smell of ammonia mixes with my blood as the anaesthesiologist tries and fails to cannulate my left hand and moves to my right.

It all becomes a bit of a blur as I try to calm myself down from a full-blown panic attack, then wonder if I could just make a run for it.

I'm covered by two blankets. Some of the nurses probably thought I was shaking from the cold. It had more to do with my previous laparoscopy to excise my endometriosis-laden being ... traumatic to say the least.

'Got it?' I say through gritted teeth as the anaesthesiologist pushes the needle further in, searching for a vein.

'Almost. You alright?'

'Sure,' I say, even though the answer doesn't really matter. This operation needs to be done.

There's a feeling of helplessness that pervades my steps in the health system, where I'm complicit in my own misery and pain through the reality that I can't do this by myself.

The needle moving underneath my skin makes me stare back at the ceiling, left hand gripping the sheets. I try to take deep breaths, forget what is happening – and when that fails, I start to spell out words in my head. It helps break the chain of thoughts before it all explodes into spiralling panic.

Of course, the first words on the call sheet are Tony Stark. T-O-N-Y-S-T-A-R-K. I probably spell it out in my head about three times before the needle hits another bad nerve and cruelly grounds me back into my body.

Then frantic reassurances race through my head, going, Hey, Tony Stark was operated on without anaesthetic, you're fine, you're fine, and, If Tony Stark can do it, you can too.

An older nurse with kind grey eyes, mask hiding her mouth, grabs my free hand. 'We're professionals. I'm not going to let anything happen to you.'

I don't know what to say, so I just ask, 'Is it done?'

'All in!' my anaesthesiologist cheers from the other side.

'Oh, thank god,' I gasp, openly crying at this point.

When I'm on the theatre table in the flimsy gown, shivering from fear and the cold now, gas mask pressed to my lips, I cling onto the older nurse.

'No more tears,' she says softly, brushing my hair back, my surrogate mum in that moment. 'Think of something wonderful and relaxing. Like the beach.'

I can see favourite scenes from Marvel movies flashing by, as well as lines of fan fiction stories I'd made up and held in my mind or posted online. My breath rasps in my ears as I stare into her eyes, trying not to just lose it, until it all fades to black, a sudden cinematic cut to the scene.

———

I have Stage 4 endometriosis, a disease that affects roughly one in nine women and takes an average of seven years to diagnose (mine took eight years). I'm in 24-7 pain, in this maddening merry-go-round that begins from the moment I open my eyes until I collapse into a medicated sleep.

This story starts a few years before though.

In 2015, I was studying my honours, concentrating on Aboriginal deaths in custody. While my endometriosis grew worse, to finally be diagnosed that year, my mental health deteriorated. I didn't know why whenever reading about police brutality, I suddenly couldn't breathe. When I saw police in public, I would end up huddled between chairs in food courts or behind cardboard advertisements, desperately trying to draw in some air and find a space I felt *safe*. With my anxiety also grew my depression, but I didn't know those terms then. I thought my brain was breaking and I didn't know why. I was terrified and ashamed, which made me silent.

Then, one day, my brother dragged me out to see a movie, my excuses for having to study falling on deaf ears.

That movie was *Avengers: Age of Ultron*. As I sat in the darkness, trying to find my breath among the crowds of strangers, the screen lit up, and as I watched the Avengers roll across the screen, with a snowy background as their canvas, I was transported to another moment. Suddenly, I wanted to understand these characters more and what made them *them*. I accomplished this later through my PhD, using the Marvel Cinematic Universe to explore fan fiction–modelled storytelling, affective engagement and guided interventions. But this piece isn't about that. It's about how this franchise and one of its characters helped me start to understand myself, the new me that I hadn't chosen, but was forming, through pain and heartache.

That moment in the cinema was the start of the MCU becoming a source of comfort for me. I began watching all of the Marvel movies I missed, immersing myself in a world that was kinder to my emotions and physical health than the real one had ever been.

Then I stumbled across *Iron Man 3*. As I watched Tony Stark go down on one knee, gasping for air and being diagnosed with a panic attack, it was a legitimate epiphany.

'That's me!' I said to the empty room, as Tony fled from his best friend, ran, ran to hide away until he felt *safe* again, safe enough to breathe. 'That's me.'

I was breathless for a different reason for the rest of the movie, tearily watching a superhero deal with what I dealt with daily. And he wasn't weird or wrong or weak. It was just one more thing that made him who he was, and he learned not only to function, but thrive. If someone like a superhero had such doubts and struggles, why couldn't I? The knowledge of what was affecting my mental health helped break my silence, allowing me to access real help.

Of course I knew this superhero and his world weren't real things to compare my life to, but it was a comfort in my struggles and gave me an 'in' to understanding these parts of myself, the ones that were new and traumatic. It's scary when you don't *know* what is making you tick, and making you break. It disconnects you from the world in a terrifying way, because it makes you feel you can't even trust yourself. A stranger, one you are forced to live as. I always felt indebted to the character of Tony Stark for helping me start connecting with these new, bruised parts of myself. I used this character to help me understand and get through my panic.

And my pain.

My fight to get my endometriosis diagnosis wasn't an easy one, so I was going to take all the help I could get. When facing ill treatment at hospitals because of my Indigeneity, or being a woman, I could immerse myself in the MCU until everything hurt a little less. In the really bad moments, when I was told over and over and over again that the pain was in my head, when I began to doubt my mind's truth, I would write gentle fan fiction stories in my head, sometimes posting online. *Something* so I could just turn off, even for a few minutes, to the way my life was stacking up, unbearable to look at sometimes, let alone to live.

Then, when a doctor did a scan, where finally, *finally* the endometriosis was seen, my organs fused together with this disease that was apparently all in my mind, I felt *seen* in the way I had when I first realised I had panic attacks. My story, the one of pain and suffering that I'd been telling the health professionals for years, was *true*, true in a way the ones in my head never could be.

This revelation led me to that theatre room for my third laparoscopy, with an endometriosis specialist. I believed in myself this time when I said it had grown back, refusing to be told any different, because I knew this story and I wasn't going to reprise my previous role. I was taking a newer one in this sequel, one where, because of her character arc in the first, the woman now believes in herself.

And while I use Tony Stark and my love of the MCU to talk myself through traumatic times, thanks to the ramifications of my disease having been left untreated for far too long, my life isn't going to be an easy-viewing movie ending wrapped up in a bow. You see, endometriosis is incurable. The medical profession still isn't sure what causes it, or even what it is. As the endometrial-like tissue grows outside of the uterus, it forms its own painful nervous systems that become inflamed, bleed and damage the tissue around them. So much scar tissue has formed over the years that, for the foreseeable future, my bowel will remain attached to my uterus. I don't get an operation where I wake up and everything is fine, where I'm cured, or pain free.

I have woken up *better* from that last laparoscopy. Sometimes, when you're in devastating, continual pain, that can be enough: *better* is a huge margin. Other times, when I can't stand up without crying in pain, *better* feels such a long way off feeling *good*.

I do physiotherapy and exercise every day, working through more pain, in the hopes that in six to twelve months, I wake up slightly better again. As I type this, my hands are shaking because to try to slow the growth of the disease (postpone the return of the supervillain, if you will, who *just won't die damnit*), I tried another hormonal pill. But, my body being my body, I had another allergic reaction to it, violently throwing up while feeling manic and distressed in ways that can be ineffable.

So many doctors have told me that I'm going to have to accept that I'll have a 'reasonable' amount of pain every day. I don't know what they think is reasonable; I know what I think is, but it isn't necessarily a place I'll reach. Living with a 'reasonable' amount of pain, well, it's very easy to say, but much harder to live.

Nothing's shiny like the endings I made up in my head. I know that logically, but sometimes I still find myself waiting, for when I emerge victorious, stronger than I ever was before. I'm realising, though, the longer I go on, I can't wait: I have to live.

But that's really hard to figure out how to do. Right now, I don't know how to be in this world as I am. I still don't understand exactly how to play the role of a Barkindji woman with endometriosis to a satisfaction level that makes me happy in my life, despite the years of rehearsals. All I know is that when it all hurts too much, I curl up and amuse myself with tales of how Tony Stark learned to work without his suit, so that just him, in all his damaged glory, was the victor at the end. Then I stagger up, take a shower, listen to music with my dad, or watch *Supernatural* with my mum.

I know I'm not Tony Stark; I'm not living my best life despite being kicked down multiple times. I don't feel brave or strong; I feel fallible and small, trying to understand how I emerged into this life I didn't choose *with* this disease attached to my side. And if that means using a fictional character and universe that have

Emergence

helped me to understand myself, break my silences and fight for fair and real diagnoses, then so be it. Because I'm a fighter, and any fighter knows you use every weapon you've got in your arsenal to survive and, eventually, to *live*.

About the Authors

Nina Angstmann is a medical doctor. Though her writing experience to date is limited to academic journal articles, when she hangs up her stethoscope she dreams of dabbling in crime fiction. She lives with her four children, three dogs and her partner, who encourages her to write and play music. This piece was compiled from a wad of contemporaneous jottings recorded on Post-it Notes over the years.

——

Chenturan Aran is a Sri Lankan Tamil Australian playwright and journalist. His plays have been performed at Melbourne Theatre Company and La Boite Theatre. His work explores memory, reconnecting with ancestral culture, migrant families and forgiveness. Chenturan has also been published by *The Age*, SBS, South Asian Today, SAARI and All The Best Radio. In 2021, Chenturan became a member of the Besen Writers Group at Malthouse Theatre. He also performs regularly in the Melbourne underground rap scene, under the name 'Chen Be Quiet'.

Emergence

Alexander Luke Burton (he/him) is a geography PhD candidate at the University of Tasmania, an island local, and purportedly a 'conscientious young man'. His main passion is to educate about the climate crisis from a social angle, and he has written about experiences of apocalypse and the desire for escape. Creative writing is a comfort from Alex's childhood, and is his secret, sustaining life source in a professional life of high stakes and high anxieties.

———

Alex Chan is an Australian-Chinese writer who grew up travelling between Melbourne and Kuala Lumpur. After completing her music degree, she returned to her first love of fiction and began writing stories. Through her work, she explores a range of themes, with a particular interest in dissecting the experience of multi-cultural and multi-hyphenate identities, drawing inspiration from her own life as an Australian-Chinese woman with familial ties to Malaysia. Alex currently resides in Melbourne with her partner and their recently adopted rescue cat.

Dahlia Eissa is a lawyer of Egyptian origin who has worked with the United Nations to increase women's participation in decision making. After 9/11 in New York, she handled anti-Arab discrimination cases, then did a stint running a French bistrot. Discovering a passion for food and wine, she unearthed her creative side. So when scleroderma put an end to her legal career, she wrote, for the joy it brings her, and to break the silence that serves oppression. Dahlia loves to travel, especially to places where she can sleep to the sound of lapping waves. She is not a morning person.

———

Monikka Eliah is an Assyrian-Australian writer and performer from Fairfield, NSW. She has participated in the National Theatre of Parramatta's Page to Stage program, CuriousWorks Breakthrough screen writing program, Co-curious and Netflix On The Brightside screenwriting program and STC's Rough Draft. Her work has been published in SBS Voices, *Runway Journal, Southerly, Kill Your Darlings, The Lifted Brow, Meanjin* and *The Saturday Paper*, and a number of anthologies. She received Southlands Breakthrough Award 2018, Wheeler Centre Playwright Hot Desk Fellowship 2020, Ausco Resilience Grant 2021, Wheeler Centre Next Chapter Award 2022 and was runner up in the SBS Emerging Writers' Competition 2022. She has presented work at the NSW Writers Centre, Wollongong Writers Festival, Sydney Writers Festival, NYW Festival, National Play Festival, WITS Festival Fatale and Sydney Festival. She is currently a member of Sydney Theatre Company's Emerging Writers Group.

Elena Filipczyk is an autistic German-Australian writer, activist and scholar. Her writing centres on her personal experiences of autism, disability, trauma and grief. Her academic work focuses on animal rights, intersectional feminism and disability.

———

Grace Huang is currently based in Chippendale, Gadi/Sydney. She grew up in North Parramatta, spending her weekends being shuttled between tutoring and her parents' furniture store. She is interested in unlikely stories – the stories of those who rarely feature as the main characters in our books, films and television. In her day job, she is an environmental lawyer working to protect the people and places we love.

———

Dr Allanah Hunt is a Barkindji woman passionate about all things writing. She has won several awards, including the inaugural *Boundless* mentorship and a *Next Chapter* fellowship, and received the Queensland Premier's Young Publishers and Writers Literary Award for her body of work so far. In her PhD, she explored affective learning, ownership of women's bodies and Unremarked Whiteness, inserting an original Indigenous female superhero into the Marvel Cinematic Universe. She has written about Aboriginal deaths in custody, mental health and now her disease of endometriosis. She loves watching her favourite Marvel movies while surrounded by her cats!

Miranda Jakich: Until now, Miranda's short stories have featured her migrant family's resettlement experience and the cultural conflict that flowed from that. This is her first story about an entirely different challenge, one that presented itself recently, starting as a secret and now fully emerged.

Sangeetha Jesudason: Noisy, colourful and rather a lot. Firm believer in joyous, dopamine-soaked fashion and pockets as a tool of female empowerment. A great deal of snorty laughter, sunshine and pear cider. Forever on the lookout for breathtaking prose. Always, ALWAYS room for a cheese plate.

Raelee Lancaster is a Brisbane-based writer and library officer whose work promotes empathy, listening and laughter. Raelee's writing has featured in *The Guardian*, SBS Voices, *Overland*, *Meanjin*, *The Big Issue*, and more. In 2018, Raelee was awarded first place for the Nakata Brophy Prize for Young Indigenous Writers. In 2019, Raelee was a recipient of a Copyright Agency First Nations Fellowship. Since 2019, Raelee has been working in the academic library sector and has a keen interest in archival research, Indigenous data sovereignty, and collections management. Raised on Awabakal land, Raelee is descended from the Wiradjuri and Biripi peoples.

Nadia Mahjouri is a Moroccan-Australian mother of five from nipaluna, lutruwita. She is a writer, group facilitator and counsellor, specialising in perinatal mental health. Her writing has been shortlisted for The Deborah Cass Prize and the Queensland Writers Centre Publishable Competition, and she is the recipient of a 2022 Arts Tasmania ASA Mentorship. Currently, she is editing her first novel, *The Half Truth*.

———

KT Major was born and raised in Singapore before moving to Sydney in 2013. She studied communications, drama and performance at Nanyang Technological University. In her first year dipping into Australia's literary scene, KT won the 2022 Peter Cowan 600 Short Story Competition in the novice category, and placed in the top 30 for the SBS Emerging Writers' Competition. Her short stories were published in the *Grieve 2022* and *BAD Western Sydney* anthologies. KT is working on a crime novel that mixes genres and incorporates her experiences from Asia and Australia. She writes mostly when her son, JM, is asleep.

———

Seth Malacari (he/they) is a queer trans man from Boorloo. They are an award-winning writer, the founder of Get YA Words Out and former chair of LoveOzYA. He is the contributing editor of the upcoming anthology *An Unexpected Party* (2023) and their work appears in *Underdog: LoveOzYA Short Stories* (2019). He has a Masters in Writing from Deakin University, specialising in Queer YA.

———

Hannah McPierzie is a teacher of students with disabilities, living in Perth, Western Australia. Hannah became deafblind after life-saving brain surgery in 2021. She is passionate about accessibility and is embarking on a new career advocating for inclusion across the community. Hannah is currently writing a book detailing her experience moving from the able-bodied world into the smaller world of disability. She is working on making the second world much bigger for all those who come after her.

Adrian Mouhajer is a non-binary lesbian Muslim Lebanese poet from Lakemba who explores themes of queerness, love, desire, family and cultural connection within their work. They are a member of Sweatshop Literacy Movement and won Highly Commended in the 2021 Sydney Opera House Antidote Mentorship for Diverse Emerging Writers. Their work has been published with *SBS Voices*, *Aniko Press* and *Diversity Arts Australia*. Adrian's work was also shortlisted in the 2022 SBS Emerging Writers' Competition. They also perform their poetry in local spaces, including the Sydney Opera House and Bankstown Arts Theatre. Adrian is the editor of *Stories Out West*, an anthology of LGBTQ+ writers of colour with a connection to Western Sydney.

———

Helen Nguyen is a Vietnamese-Australian writer from West Melbourne and a member of Sweatshop Literacy Movement. Her writing has been published by SBS Voices, Sydney Opera House, Pedestrian TV, Storycasters and will appear in Sweatshop's upcoming anthology *Povo*. She is currently a TedXSydney Youth Curator and intern at the United Nations Office of Higher Commissioner of Human Rights. Helen is in her final year of a Bachelor of Law and Communication (Creative Writing). She is expected to be admitted as a legal practitioner in 2024.

Sidney Norris is an author, composer and poet – an unemployable hat-trick of artistic self-loathing. His past ventures range from the independent distribution of his own comic book, to touring internationally in an alternative rock band. His work often highlights the patriarchal ills that misshape the mental health of boys and men. He has a Bachelor of Arts Screen: Production from the Australian Film Television and Radio School, and is currently studying a Bachelor of Music (Composition) at the Sydney Conservatorium of Music. When he's not braving autobiographical depths, Sid can be found in the present with his impeccable wife, Erin.

Saneia Norton is a public servant turned entrepreneur, landscape architect and design communication specialist. At the NSW Government Architect's Office, she designed projects from Circular Quay to Broken Hill, until a series of mid-career speed bumps became the catalyst for reinvention. Saneia left behind the cubicles and cardigans of government to launch the design communication company SNDC, helping design professionals wield words as powerfully as images, build confidence in presenting work and move beyond long-held scars of brutal design juries. Saneia hosts the podcast Dig Beneath Design, sharing the best communication tips from top designers.

Taymin-lee Pagett is a queer Indigenous writer from the South Coast. Taymin has been writing and curating poetry since she was fourteen years old. She carries passion for all the arts, through all its mediums, with particular interest in illustration and film. Taymin may be found sitting in her favourite bar, strolling a local art exhibition or at a local gig.

———

Geetha Pathanjali was born and raised in Naarm in a Tamil Sri Lankan migrant family. She writes predominantly for her twelve-year-old self, who is overjoyed that she is finally stepping into the bracing waters of storytelling again. Outside of writing, Geetha works in urban policy and is an advocate for creating equitable cities.

———

Betty Petrov took thirty years to finally write the story she always wanted to tell. A first-generation Australian who grew up in the western suburbs of Melbourne, Betty was born to immigrant parents who taught her the value of resilience and determination. She hopes her story will inspire others to find their own voice and tell their own story.

Tessa Piper was born and raised in Sydney's eastern suburbs and now lives in Melbourne's inner west. She acknowledges the First Peoples of Australia as the traditional owners of the land on which she lives and the first storytellers. Tessa has degrees in physiology, public health and health management. She is currently studying creative writing. Tessa has dedicated her career to health, social policy and human rights reforms that address discrimination and promote fairness, equity and opportunity. She is a very proud mum to her two children, Bailey and Asher, and her very naughty beagle, Donut. The 2022 SBS Emerging Writers' Competition is the first writing competition she has ever entered.

———

Hope Sneddon is a final year PhD student at RMIT focusing on finance cultures and memoir writing. She holds an MA from the University of Zurich majoring in Literature Studies. She has written creative and academic works for various publications, including the Australian Multilingual Writing Project and the *EAAS Women's Network Journal*. When she isn't working on her writing, you can find Hope hiking in nature. She dedicates this story to her brother and father, taken too soon.

Gemma Tamock is a performer, director, writer and English as a Second Language teacher. She has directed opera, music theatre and theatre for young people over a number of years. She has written *Anansi's Web* for the stage and two short documentary films, *Whitewash* and *A Black Bird*, based on her South Sea Islander heritage.

———

Charaf Tartoussi is an award-winning spoken word poet based in Naarm. Her work has appeared in several publications and has seen her featured in festivals around the country. She draws primarily on her own experiences as a Muslim first-generation Australian. 'beyond the cloth' is her first attempt at memoir.

———

Zoë Amanda Wilson is a professional stunt performer and full-time honours student who chose to dabble in memoir-writing while procrastinating on a Cognitive Psychology lab report. This will be her first published work, as long as you don't count pithy Facebook statuses. When she's not up to her eyeballs in coursework or literally on fire, Zoë enjoys sewing, riding her motorcycle, playing the drums, rock climbing, cheerleading, running a book club and starting at least one new hobby every month.